SANTA
ASSIGNMENT
DELORES FOSSEN

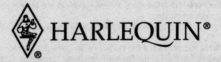

HARLEQUIN®

TORONTO • NEW YORK • LONDON
AMSTERDAM • PARIS • SYDNEY • HAMBURG
STOCKHOLM • ATHENS • TOKYO • MILAN • MADRID
PRAGUE • WARSAW • BUDAPEST • AUCKLAND

ISBN 0-373-22812-0

SANTA ASSIGNMENT

ABOUT THE AUTHOR

Imagine a family tree that includes Texas cowboys, Choctaw and Cherokee Indians, a Louisiana pirate and a Scottish rebel who battled side by side with William Wallace. With ancestors like that, it's easy to understand why Texas author and former air force captain Delores Fossen feels as if she was genetically predisposed to writing romances. Along the way to fulfilling her DNA destiny, Delores married an air force top gun who just happens to be of Viking descent. With all those romantic bases covered, she doesn't have to look too far for inspiration.

Books by Delores Fossen

HARLEQUIN INTRIGUE
648—HIS CHILD
679—A MAN WORTH REMEMBERING
704—MARCHING ORDERS
727—CONFISCATED CONCEPTION
788—VEILED INTENTIONS
812—SANTA ASSIGNMENT

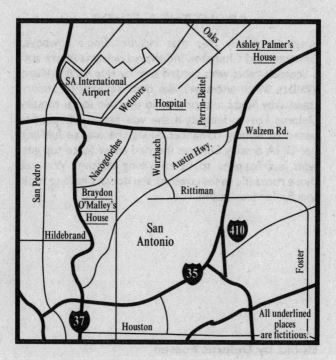

All underlined places are fictitious.

CAST OF CHARACTERS

Lieutenant Brayden O'Malley—San Antonio Police Department. To save his young son, Brayden asks his former sister-in-law, Ashley, to have his child.

Ashley Palmer—Once a rising star among criminal defense attorneys, for the past two and a half years she's been hiding from a vicious stalker. However, to save her nephew, she's willing to risk everything to have Brayden's baby.

Colton O'Malley—Brayden's three-year-old son and Ashley's nephew. He's too young to realize the sacrifices Ashley and his father are willing to make for him.

Miles Granville—Ashley's former boyfriend. He's jealous of Brayden and Ashley's relationship, and is holding an old grudge, since Ashley once defended the two men who tried to kill him.

Trevor Chapman—Once Ashley's close friend. Is Trevor hiding behind a timid facade, and is he the stalker who's been tormenting her?

Hyatt Chapman—A fugitive who blames Ashley for his felony conviction.

To my editors, Denise O'Sullivan and Stacy Boyd.
Thanks for everything.

Prologue

Northern Virginia

He'd found her.

Finally.

And that meant now he could kill her.

From across the street, he watched Ashley Palmer as she parked her dark blue compact in her driveway. Since there was no garage, she stepped out in plain view. Practically right in front of him.

Yes, it was Ashley all right. A different hair color. But definitely her.

She turned—not in his direction, though—and ducked her head down slightly, probably to shelter her face from the angry December wind. A few stray snowflakes swirled through the air, some landing on her hat and scarf. Her breath created a filmy cloud around her face.

Her footsteps slowed as she approached her house, and she examined the other vehicle parked in front. Not his. But a rental, driven there by a visitor

who was probably the last person on earth she expected to see today.

Well, the second to the last anyway.

He almost certainly had the honor of being at the very bottom on that theoretical list. But he had no plans for her to see him.

Not until he was actually in the process of killing her, that is.

He smiled. The thoughts of her death sent a rush of pleasure and anticipation through him. It wouldn't be fast. Not some impulsive act born out of rage and the need for vengeance. It would be methodical. Precise. Cold-blooded. Because she had to be punished for what she'd done, and a quick bullet to the head wouldn't punish her enough.

No.

Not *nearly* enough.

He'd made a mistake when he'd killed her sister, Dana. But he'd learned a lot from that little faux pas. Without suffering, retribution just wasn't very satisfying. This time, there would definitely be suffering.

In fact, he'd already set his plan of suffering into motion with the *surprise* he had left in her house while she was out. It'd been easy to disarm the security system and slip inside. And his gift would perhaps rid her of any peace of mind she'd managed to find since her sister's death.

Sweet, delicious torture. With the promise of much more to come.

But for now, he watched.

Waited.

And savored the scene that was unfolding right in front of him. He resisted the urge to open the van window so the heavily tinted glass wouldn't obstruct his view of her and the encounter that was about to take place.

Pausing at the bottom of the steps, she stared up at the tall imposing visitor in the black coat who stood on her front porch. Even through the tinted glass of his car window, he could see Ashley's expression go from astonishment to concern.

He laughed.

Because he knew that concern would only get worse, much worse, when she learned why her former brother-in-law, Lt. Brayden O'Malley, had come all the way from San Antonio. It was a stroke of luck, really. A special kind of torment for both of them that even he couldn't have planned.

Not only had the lieutenant indirectly led him to Ashley—through the PI the man had hired to check up on her—but Brayden O'Malley would be the one to deliver the first blow. Or maybe the second, if she found the little surprise first. But it definitely wouldn't be the last.

No. He would do the final deed himself.

After he'd played with her for a while.

He laughed at that thought, too. And he settled back into the seat, turned up the volume on his eavesdropping equipment and waited for Ashley Palmer's world to come crashing down around her.

Chapter One

"Did hell freeze over?" Ashley asked, stepping onto the porch.

She spared him a glance, barely, before she turned her back to him and pulled out a key ring from her black leather shoulder purse. A tiny canister of pepper spray dangled from the large brass ring and clanged against the keys.

Brayden took a deep steadying breath. It didn't help. Of course, that was asking a lot from a mere breath. Not much would steady him at this point. Especially not coming face-to-face, or rather face-to-back, with a woman he'd vowed never to lay eyes on again.

He'd made that vow exactly two years, seven months and four days ago. At a moment when Ashley still had his dead wife's blood on her hands—both literally and figuratively. But Brayden had to push aside those brutal images. While he was at it, he had to dismiss the vow he'd made.

Because he desperately needed her.

Of course, now he had to figure out how to tell her that he wanted to take her seemingly ordered life and turn it upside down. Oh, and that the upside-down part would include forging a highly intimate, permanent relationship with a man she hated—him.

Whatever the opposite of a piece of cake was, this was it.

"Maybe hell did freeze over," Brayden admitted under his breath. "Because I could swear there was just a sharp drop in the temperature."

He obviously didn't mumble it nearly low enough because Ashley glanced over her shoulder at him. The corner of her peach-tinged mouth lifted. Not from humor. Nope. There wasn't a trace of fun and merriment on that mouth or in her cool turquoise-blue eyes.

So that she could reach the lock on the door, Ashley stepped closer. Close enough for him to catch her scent.

Something exotic and high priced.

A reminder that his former sister-in-law had expensive tastes, even if she no longer lived in luxury. This modest one-story place was a far cry from her sprawling upscale house in San Antonio.

Ditto for her present job. According to the background check he'd had run on her, she was practicing law—but mainly pro bono cases—for single mothers trying to collect overdue child support. Not exactly a six-figure income, and it was a huge finan-

cial step down from being the rising star of criminal defense attorneys in San Antonio.

"Come inside before you get frostbite or something," Ashley said, shifting the paper sack of groceries to her hip so she could open the door. The security system immediately began to whine, and she reached inside to press the buttons on a keypad to disarm it.

Like her pseudosmile, her words weren't really an invitation. Definitely not driven by a need to be polite, they were no doubt a product of curiosity. But he sensed apprehension as well. Lots of that.

Brayden understood completely.

Every inch of him was apprehensive.

She set the bag on a counter that separated the tiny living area from the dining room and peeled off her burgundy leather coat and hat. She'd cut her hair. Short and fashionably unstyled. And it was no longer honey-blond, but a dark chocolate that was a startling contrast against her cool pale skin. And surprisingly attractive.

Brayden truly wished he hadn't noticed.

It had to be the fatigue and the stress.

It *had* to be.

"I'm not sure how this should work," Ashley admitted, moistening those peachy lips. "Do we try some chitchat first? Or should we just get straight to the point of the argument that we both know we'll end up having?"

His former sister-in-law had faults, but her directness sure wasn't one of them. Under the circumstances, he found it refreshing.

"Let's skip the chitchat. And just to let you know up front—brace yourself because you're not going to like the *point*," he volunteered.

"I figured as much." She propped her hands on her hips. Not waif hips either. Curved ones. She was definitely built like a woman, and the snug jeans only emphasized that.

Yet something else he wished he hadn't noticed.

Ashley studied him a moment. "So, you found out, huh?"

Brayden was almost certain he blinked. He hadn't thought she would be the one delivering the surprises today. "Found out? About what?"

She blinked too. And for a split second, there was a panicky look in Ashley's eyes. But she quickly covered it with a huff, which had a definite *duh* tone to it. "About where to find me, of course. Let me guess—you want to confront me about your unresolved anger? And this is some kind of requirement for a twelve-step program to help you deal with Dana's murder?"

"No twelve-step program could help with that." It'd taken long agonizing months to push the pain of his wife's death aside just so he could function. It'd taken longer still for the numbness to go away. And even now, his life wasn't normal. Never would be.

"Well, yeah," she grumbled. "You got me there."

Ashley turned her back to him again, pulled a pint of caramel-fudge ice cream from her grocery bag and strolled toward the fridge. She tried to look nonchalant—distant, even—but her tight at-war jaw muscles gave her away. This was no proverbial piece of cake for her, either. Especially since she'd let something slip. *So, you found out, huh?*

Brayden would let that pass.

For now.

Ashley took out a spoon from one of the drawers and opened the ice cream. "Wow, this must really be something earth-shattering for you not to get right to the *point.* You're not the beating-around-the-bush type." She sampled the caramel-fudge, made a sound of approval and recapped the carton.

"This isn't easy." Man, what an understatement. Brayden shook his head and wished he'd at least practiced what to say. He'd interrogated serial killers and hadn't felt this uncomfortable.

"So, why don't we just start with you telling me how you found me?" she prompted. "I've changed my name and kept my address a secret, so I seriously doubt you just happened to be in the neighborhood."

"I hired a private investigator to find you."

"A PI? This must be important." Ashley had already reached for the freezer door, but she paused just a second before she opened it carefully as if the

handle were fragile and might shatter in her hand. "So just how important is it?"

"Very. It's Colton." It was all he could manage to say without taking another breath.

Her gaze rifled to his. She stuffed the ice cream in the freezer, slammed the door and went toward him. Not slowly this time. Her long strides quickly ate up the space between, and she stopped only a few feet away.

"What happened?" she asked. "Has he been hurt?"

Brayden was thankful for the true concern that went through her eyes. The only real connection he had left to Ashley was through Colton. His three-year-old son. And her nephew. It was that connection that had brought him to her.

He was prepared to beg if necessary.

"He wasn't hurt," Brayden explained. "He's had some medical problems." A simple almost sterile explanation. It still put his stomach in knots.

Ashley reached out as if to touch him but immediately withdrew her hand and crammed it into her back jeans' pocket. "Will I need to sit down before I hear the rest of this?" she asked.

"Possibly."

Another nod that was edgy and clipped, and she dragged out not one but two chairs from beneath the small tiled table. Brayden didn't take her up on her nonverbal gesture to sit. He continued to stand even after she dropped down into the seat.

"The diagnosis is acute lymphocytic leukemia," he went on, after another breath.

She made a small helpless sound and pressed her fingertips to her mouth. "Oh, God. Leukemia. How he is? Is he okay?"

No. His son wasn't *okay.* But Brayden didn't even try to get that out. "He's had chemo and is stabilized for now. But he needs a bone-marrow transplant. Not immediately. But eventually."

"Okay." She pulled in her breath, hard, and repeated that one word several times. "So, you need me to be tested to see if I'm a match—"

"You're not a match," he explained. "You're already in the bone-marrow registry so Colton's doctors were able to check. That's not why I'm here."

That brought Ashley slowly back to her feet. "Then why did you come?"

It was a good question, and Brayden considered a detailed, clinical answer. One that would make her at least think about his proposition before she tossed him out the door.

But there was no way to make this clinical.

Tears shimmered in her eyes. "Mercy, you're not here to tell me he's not going to make it—"

"Colton needs a sibling donor," he interrupted, not wanting her to finish that thought. Then, he paused. Waiting to see if she had a response. She didn't. Ashley just stared at him. "A sibling with my DNA. And his mother's."

She shook her head. Maybe because she didn't un-understand what he was asking, or God forbid, maybe because she was already saying no.

She *couldn't* say no.

He couldn't lose his son.

He just couldn't.

"I'm asking you to have a baby," he explained.

Ashley blinked back the tears, and her eyes widened. "You're…what?"

He swallowed hard and with it swallowed what little pride he had left.

Which wasn't much.

"I'm asking you to have a baby," Brayden clarified. "Our baby."

FROM THE MOMENT Ashley had seen Brayden O'Malley standing on her front porch, she'd imagined lots of things he might say to her.

But this sure wasn't one of them.

Not even close.

Still reeling from the news of her nephew's illness, this latest addition to the conversation caused a serious information overload.

"*Our* baby?" Ashley repeated, certain she'd misunderstood him.

"Our baby," he verified.

The words seemed to stick in his throat. And probably did. After all, he was talking to *her*. They weren't friends. In fact, the last thing Brayden had said to her

two years, seven months and four days ago was that he hoped like hell he never saw her face again.

She'd given him that. Ashley had disappeared from his life. From her nephew's.

From her own life.

"The doctors think a sibling donor is Colton's best chance for a bone marrow match," Brayden continued. "Because the DNA will be similar."

So, she'd heard him correctly. Her nephew had leukemia and needed a bone marrow transplant. She and her former brother-in-law were the best bet for giving him that.

Oh, mercy.

When the full impact of that hit her, her heart landed somewhere in the vicinity of her knees. And because she didn't want to risk something as dignity-reducing as her legs giving way, Ashley sat back down.

"It's not a hundred percent," Brayden went on. "I mean, nothing is. But at least this way there's a fighting chance we'll have a suitable donor. No one in my family matched. I've even contacted all of your relatives, including distant cousins. No luck. And there's not a match in the international bone marrow registry, either."

"Oh, mercy." Ashley searched for whatever she was supposed to say in a situation like this and came up with a total blank. "A lawyer without an immediate opinion. That's one for the record."

"Well, this isn't an everyday occurrence." He

groaned, scrubbed his hands over his face and tipped his eyes toward the ceiling as if seeking divine guidance. "I should have found a better way to say it."

"Trust me, there was no better way to say what you just said. Besides, you got your point across— believe me. A baby," Ashley mumbled, aware that by repeating it, she was starting to sound a little psychotic. "Fate sure has a twisted sense of humor, huh?"

He shrugged. And made a sound of agreement. A mild sound. Which wasn't congruent with his rigid posture. In that calf-length black coat with a dark blue suit beneath it and with his conservative, short, bronze-colored hair, Brayden looked much like a judge or a military officer standing at attention.

Or perhaps waiting for a firing squad.

"I know it's a lot to ask…especially since you have a new life here."

"A new life not by choice," Ashley reminded him, lifting her index finger in a let's-not-forget-that-little-detail gesture. "But out of necessity."

He nodded. "Because of the stalker."

Oh, yes. Always the stalker.

A person who might or might not be her former client, Hyatt Chapman. A name that even now caused her lungs to tighten and her breath to go thin. The sociopathic slime, whoever he was, had given her some of the most terrifying and troubling moments of her life—excluding her sister's death.

And this, of course.

This definitely qualified as troubling.

Ironically, it was easier to talk to Brayden about a crazed stalker who had threatened, and tried to kill her than it was to discuss her nephew's illness or a possible baby. So, Ashley let her mouth go where her brain was already gladly leading her. "I haven't received any threatening letters or calls since I changed my name and moved here."

Another nod. "That's good."

The words were right, but Brayden's body language added an important postscript to it. It was *good* that the stalker hadn't found her, but if—and that was a huge if—she considered what he'd just asked her to consider, it would almost certainly mean her coming out of hiding.

It would also probably mean having to deal with the stalker all over again.

Oh, mercy.

Ashley wasn't sure she was ready for round two. Round one had nearly killed her.

"And I really have started over here," she continued, talking more to herself than to him. "I mean, I'm doing something that matters."

For once in her life.

Of course, that was the problem with doing something that mattered. It didn't automatically exclude other things that mattered, too.

Like her nephew.

But a baby? This was no easy fix. No easy choice.

Brayden walked closer, hovered over her a moment and sank down onto the chair across from her. Directly across. The knees of his pants brushed against her jeans.

His gaze met hers. And there it was. That shock of stunning green. She'd almost forgotten all those tones of vibrant color in his eyes.

Almost.

What she hadn't almost forgotten was his face. Ruggedly handsome by anyone's standards. Good Celtic cheekbones. A naturally tanned complexion. Toned and lean.

He was thirty-three now and had tiny lines at the corners of his eyes. Character lines, people called them. As if he needed any more character on that face.

Brayden pulled his gaze from hers. Shook his head. Mumbled something indistinguishable. And rammed his hands into both sides of his hair. "I wouldn't have asked if—"

"If it weren't for Colton," Ashley finished. "Oh, I *really* do know that. I can only imagine what it cost you to come here today."

Eye contact again. Barely a glance, though. He even cleared his throat. In the six-plus years she'd known Brayden O'Malley, she'd never heard him clear his throat. Ditto for any nervous gestures. The Rock of Gibraltar, Dana had called him. But today, Ashley was seeing a very different side of the Rock. The edges were definitely crumbling a bit.

"And I can imagine what it's costing you to even consider it," he admitted.

Touché.

There was an understanding, maybe even a bizarre empathy, left between them after all. And of course the memories were there, too. Lots of memories. Of the old professional arguments between a dedicated homicide cop and an equally dedicated and frequent pain-in-the-ass criminal defense attorney.

And they especially had all the old arguments about Dana between them.

Well, one argument really. The one where they'd accused each other of getting Dana killed.

I hope like hell I never see your face again.

Because those words Brayden had said to her long ago just wouldn't go away, because they started to pound in her head like war drums, Ashley stood to give herself some breathing room.

"Take some time," he offered when she started to pace. "Think about it."

Ashley managed a nod. Somehow. Even though it seemed as if every muscle in her neck was knotted and stiff.

Part of her desperately wanted to jump at the chance to help her nephew. And another part of her just plain resented Brayden for bringing all of this to her.

But this wasn't just about Colton. Nor was it just about Brayden and her.

It was also about a baby.

A baby who could potentially save a child's life and complicate everything else. Because a baby was permanent. A bond. And it would mean bonding with a man who had trouble even looking her in the eye for more than a couple of seconds.

A man who couldn't forgive her.

A man who was a reminder that she couldn't forgive herself.

How could she possibly conceive a child under those circumstances?

Yet, how could she risk losing her nephew?

Pacing, repeating each of those arguments to herself, Ashley caught a glimpse of Brayden in the mirror on the antique sideboard on the other side of the table. Still stoic. Still soldier stiff.

Except for his eyes.

And in that glance Ashley realized that Brayden had the same questions, the same concerns, the same fears as she did.

"You wouldn't have to give up your life," he added. "But I know it'd change everything."

Yes. It would. Heck, it had *already* changed everything. The life she'd so carefully put together, the sanity she'd found, hadn't been shattered exactly, but it was no longer intact, either.

"I'll have think about it," Ashley assured him. But she couldn't do that with Brayden in the room. She needed time. Alone.

Mercy, where had all the air gone?

Because she was sure she was on the verge of tears, and because there was no way she wanted Brayden to see her cry, she had to get out of there.

"I'll call you," she said, making sure her tone indicated this conversation was on hold.

And she was obviously successful in getting that point across because Brayden didn't say anything, and he didn't follow her. Ashley started toward her room.

Just as she detected the smell.

Was it smoke?

Ashley turned back around. So did he. He lifted his head slightly. And it was on the tip of her tongue to ask if he'd recently had a cigarette. But it was an unnecessary question. Because Brayden didn't smoke, and besides the smell wasn't in the living room.

She spun toward the hall just off the back of the kitchen and saw her bedroom door.

And the thick black smoke oozing from beneath it.

Chapter Two

Brayden didn't waste any time.

The moment he smelled the smoke, he pushed past Ashley and raced through the kitchen, frantically searching. No smoke there, and no obvious source of fire.

"It's coming from my bedroom," Ashley informed him, pointing toward the hall.

She started ahead of him, but again, he moved around her and hurried to the room she'd pointed out. He saw the smoke drifting along the floor. And worse. Rising. It wouldn't be long before it made its way through the entire house.

He touched his palm to the door.

It wasn't hot. Thank God.

The old-fashioned faceted-glass doorknob was cool, as well. So, he opened it. Cautiously. Peering around the corner. When he was satisfied that he wasn't about to face a full-scale blaze, he gave the door a shove with his shoulder.

No backdraft or wall of fire.

That was the good news. But the bad news was there were foot-high orange-red flames on the dresser tucked into the corner, and the flames weren't staying put, either. They were quickly eating their way toward the draping lace curtains on a nearby window.

"Grab a fire extinguisher or some water," he yelled back to Ashley. "And call the fire department."

Sheltering his face from the blaze, he latched onto the curtains and ripped them down from the thick brass rod. Best not to give the fire any more fuel. It already had enough with what was left of the array of dried flowers, scented candles and pictures on the dresser.

Brayden stripped a quilt from the bed and beat down the flames. No easy task. Some scattered. There were sparks and sputters. And the black coiling smoke. It was suffocating, but he choked back a cough and kept working.

He soon realized just how lucky they'd been. It could have been worse. Much worse. If the fire had gotten just a few more minutes of a head start, they would have had an inferno on their hands, and the whole place might have gone up in flames.

"I have the extinguisher," he heard her say.

She began to spray the white foam on the small smoldering spots that had ignited around the base of the dresser and the rug on the side of the bed. Bray-

den continued to put out the heart of the blaze by pounding it with the quilt.

The picture frames shattered against the wall. The melting candles sputtered. He stomped on the partially burned dried flowers that he raked to the floor.

One of the embers from the dried flowers flew out and landed on his pant leg. He reached down to brush it off, just as one of the flames erupted back into a blaze. The spark singed his hand, and he quickly drew it back, trying to maneuver the quilt so he could smother the fire.

"Brayden!" Ashley called out. From the alarm in her voice, she must have noticed his clothes on fire. She turned the extinguisher in his direction and hosed him down.

It worked.

But Brayden didn't take the time to thank her. He returned to the tiny embers still left around the dresser and kept battling them until finally all that was left was the smoke and the damage. Minor damage at that. Yes, indeed, they'd been lucky.

"Are you hurt?" she asked.

He glanced down at the small red mark on his left hand. There'd be a blister but no real damage. "I'm fine."

She obviously didn't take his word for it. Ashley grabbed him by the wrist and checked it herself. Her touch was warm. Surprisingly gentle. Too gentle. And the examination put them too close. Prac-

tically body to body. It didn't help when her arm brushed his.

Brayden tugged his hand away and stepped back. "It's nothing," he insisted, wondering why that insistence felt as if it had a double meaning.

And why it felt like a lie.

"Should I call the fire department and tell them not to come?" Ashley asked, doing her own share of stepping back from him.

"No. They're probably already on the way, and they can make sure all the flames are fully out." For good measure, Brayden took the fire extinguisher and gave the whole area a good soaking.

Ashley went to the window, unhooked the lock and threw it open. The icy air blasted through the room, which was exactly what they needed because it helped thin the smoke almost immediately. It also shook off any lingering effects from her too-gentle touch.

"I don't understand how this happened," she said in between gulps of breath. She rubbed her hands up and down her arms. Probably from the cold, but Brayden figured part of it was a reaction to the near disaster.

Adrenaline was certainly pumping through him. As if he needed more. He'd been functioning on adrenaline and caffeine for days now.

He kept the fire extinguisher ready in case a secondary blaze reignited, and he examined the dresser.

Even though he'd knocked off the items that had been on it, he could see the residue that had pooled on the veneer finish. It looked like melted wax.

"Did you leave a candle burning?" he asked.

"No." Muffling a cough and still rubbing her arms, Ashley walked closer. "I mean, I use candles a lot, but I didn't light one today."

He stooped down and used the nozzle of the extinguisher to sort through the still-warm rubble. "You're positive? Because it looks as if one burned down and managed to catch those dried flowers on fire."

When Ashley didn't answer, Brayden looked up at her. It seemed as if she was about to say something. But then she changed her mind. Instead, she shook her head and angled her eyes in another direction. "It's possible. I guess."

He stood up and checked Ashley's recently reangled blue eyes. Nothing like Dana's pale hazel ones. In fact, for sisters, they had few physical attributes in common.

Which helped this visit considerably.

It would have been much harder if she'd reminded him of his late wife.

"What's this about?" Brayden demanded. In the distance, he could hear sirens. A welcome sound, except for the fact that he didn't want their arrival to give Ashley an excuse not to answer.

"What do you mean?" Ashley grabbed a fringed throw from the foot of the bed, slung it around her

shoulders and went back to the window. She stared out, once again diverting her gaze.

Oh, man.

That couldn't be a good sign.

"It's possible. I guess?" he said, repeating her own vague explanation. "Maybe I've been a cop too long, but that just set off the BS meter in my head."

"You're right." And that's all Ashley said for several seconds. Before she bent down and picked up a damaged picture frame from the floor. She fastened her gaze to it. "You've been a cop too long. Eleven years, huh?"

"Twelve. But if you think asking me that totally irrelevant question will distract me, think again." He went closer, caught her arm and turned her around to face him. "In fact, that's twice today you've set off that BS meter, and the first time was when you asked me the question—*so you found out, huh?* What'd you mean by that, Ashley?"

"You don't have a BS meter." She slung off his grip with far more force than required. "You have a blasted tape recorder. And if you must know, I meant nothing by it. I was simply surprised that'd you found me, that's all."

That BS meter went nuts.

Brayden would have called her on that lie if she hadn't turned the picture frame around. Even though the glass was shattered and smeared with soot, he could still see that it contained a photograph of his

son. Not a recent shot but one taken when Colton was just a couple of months old. When his son was still healthy.

Ashley had him cradled in her arms.

"I want to see him," she whispered, drawing the photograph to her chest. "I want to go to San Antonio."

Outside, the sirens howled, coming closer. But it wasn't the sirens that captured Brayden's attention. It was the woman holding the image of his son, and his future, in her hands. If this was her own version of a distraction so she wouldn't have to answer his questions, it was working.

Brayden felt a tight fist close around his heart.

It wasn't the yes he'd prayed for. But then, it wasn't a no either.

"I promised myself I wouldn't go back, ever," Ashley continued. "Not because I don't love Colton. I do. But going back…well, it could create some problems. I'm talking *huge* problems."

"I know. But I'm not asking you to leave behind what you have here. We could work that out. And the baby wouldn't be your responsibility. It'd—"

"It's not just that." She motioned toward her hair. "This isn't for cosmetic reasons, Brayden. I did *this* hoping he wouldn't find me."

"I know."

If she stepped away from this place she'd created, she could be stepping into danger. He'd already made security arrangements. He had already worked out

ways to keep her safe. Plus, he'd taken into account how to minimize the effects this might have on her life.

But there was no way to minimize everything.

No way to make this even close to perfect.

To save his son, he'd have to ask Ashley to put herself in danger.

Chapter Three

"I made the right decision to come here," Ashley mumbled under her breath.

Again.

And maybe if she repeated it often enough, she'd soon start to believe it.

Well, one could hope anyway.

"Did you say something?" the nurse asked.

Ashley shook her head, took off her coat and draped it over her forearm.

The nurse handed her a surgical mask. "Use this if you plan to make any physical contact with the patient."

The cheery yellow mask was littered with happy faces. Definitely not a reflection of Ashley's mood. She felt like one big raw nerve walking around on two-inch heels.

The five-hour trip from Springfield, Virginia, hadn't done much to soothe her. In fact, it'd done the exact opposite. Since Brayden had seemingly turned mute on the flight and subsequent drive from the air-

port to the hospital, that'd left her with way too much thinking time on her hands. Yet, she still didn't seem any closer to making a decision.

A baby, even a hypothetical one, was definitely a lot to think about.

She'd never even changed a diaper—a truly ridiculous thought. And that was the least ridiculous and stressful thought of all the what-if-I-really-do-this? thoughts zipping through her head.

For starters, a baby would require a pregnancy. Specifically her getting pregnant.

By Brayden, no less.

Even if they did the procedure through insemination, which was a certainty, it still had an intimacy to it. Then, there was the waiting and the praying that the baby's bone marrow matched Colton's. From the info Brayden had given her to read on the plane, they'd have to wait until the ninth week of pregnancy for the amnio to determine if the hypothetical baby was a donor match.

As if that weren't enough, then there was the whole *after* the amnio part. The remaining seven months of pregnancy. The delivery.

And especially the part after that.

The part that was still one gigantic blur in her head even though those five hours had given her plenty of time to dwell on it.

Ashley decided to let it stay a blur for a while. It seemed a wussy response, but a blur was the most she

could handle right now. She'd have to think about it tomorrow, especially since she was within moments of seeing her nephew.

"If you'll come this way," the nurse instructed, "I'll take you to Colton's room."

Ashley followed her and glanced around the hall. "We aren't waiting for Brayden?"

"He's still in with the doctors. He said he'll join you when he's finished."

Okay. So she hadn't expected to do this alone. But in some ways, it might be easier. Of course, she could say that about a lot of things that involved Brayden. Being around him had a unique way of unnerving her.

The nurse pushed open the door and led Ashley inside. Not the drab gray interior she'd expected but one with a brightly colored jungle mural. Taped to the wall were childlike drawings of what appeared to be Santa and some rather lopsided gifts. A miniature Christmas tree was sitting on the table beneath the drawings.

Ashley spotted Brayden's sister, Katelyn, in a chair in the corner, and they exchanged silent but amicable greetings before Ashley turned toward the hospital bed.

There were machines, their screens registering various data with thready almost frantic jolts of movement. One of them was making a soft pulsing sound. And in the center of that was her nephew. Dana's son.

He was so small.

That was her first reaction. Followed by what felt like a heavyweight's fist to her solar plexus. Ashley actually had to catch onto the nurse's arm.

"Do you need a moment?" the nurse whispered.

Ashley waved her off and forced herself to let go of the woman. Colton certainly didn't need a visit from a wimp.

She took a few short deep breaths, moistened her lips, pulled back her shoulders and approached him. At the sound of her heels clicking on the tile floor, Colton's eyes fluttered open, zooming right in on her.

Ashley had seen those green eyes before. Brayden's eyes. It stirred at least a dozen new emotions just seeing them on a child she loved completely and unconditionally.

Many of those doubts and blurs evaporated. And Ashley knew. She'd made the right decision to come here. No matter what else happened, this was the right thing to do.

"Are you one of Santa's helpers?" Colton asked, his voice sleepy. He had a blue dog-eared bunny tucked in the crook of his arm.

Ashley glanced down at her garnet-red pants and sweater. The outfit definitely had a holiday look to it. She smiled. She didn't have to force it, either, even though her facial muscles felt a little out of practice. It'd been a while since she had smiled.

Two years, seven months and four days.

Much too long.

He smiled, too. Wow! What a face. Pure innocence cut with just the right amount of mischief. It broke her heart and warmed it at the same time.

"Nope. I'm afraid I'm not Santa's helper. Sorry." She sat in the chair next to his bed. "I'm your Aunt Ashley."

"I got another aunt. Aunt Katelyn. Are you a cop like her?" He held up the fake "rookie-in-training" badge he'd had tucked in the covers.

"Nope. I'm sort of a bad guy. I'm a lawyer."

His eyes widened. "Like my mom was?"

Oh, mercy. That put a lump in her throat. "Yep. Like your mom." Because she wasn't supposed to get too close, Ashley resisted touching those soft golden-brown curls that lay tousled on his forehead. "So, you want to be a cop when you grow up?"

"Sure. Like my daddy."

"Good choice. He's the best of the best. And I should know. I used to have to cross-examine him in court. He could be a real pain in the…neck."

Colton giggled, as if he'd known what she'd almost let slip. But the giggle faded when his attention drifted to the machines surrounding him. "Did you come to visit me 'cause I'm sick?"

"That's one of the reasons." That required another deep breath. "But you'll get better."

"Dad says that, too. So do Grandma and Grandpa. And Aunt Katelyn and Uncle Garrett."

Garrett. Brayden's brother. Another cop. And yet someone else she'd routinely clashed with during

her power attorney days. She doubted she'd receive any warm nonverbal greetings from Garrett O'Malley the way she had from Katelyn. Still, Ashley wouldn't let that put a damper on this moment.

Colton cupped his hand around his mouth and lowered his voice. "I don't want to be in the hospital for Christmas. There's no chimney, and Santa might not be able to find me here."

That brought on more than a lump in her throat. It was an entire boulder. "Oh, Santa will find you all right," Ashley said, speaking around that boulder. "I'm a lawyer, remember—I'll subpoena him or something. Besides, it's two weeks until Christmas, and you might be home by then."

He shrugged, apparently not sure he believed that. Ashley silently cursed. Three years old was much too young to lose hope.

Maybe twenty-nine was, too.

For some reason, looking at Colton's sweet innocent face gave her hope. Ironic since she hadn't been able to find hope since Dana's death.

"Santa *will* find you," she promised. "I'll make sure of it."

She watched as he considered that with those now pensive green eyes. He gave a little satisfied nod. "Can you make it snow, too?"

Ashley laughed. "I'll see what I can do, but since we're in San Antonio, we might have to settle for the fake stuff. Is that okay?"

"Okay." Colton shifted his gaze in the direction of the door. "Daddy," he said, grinning.

Brayden was there, in the doorway. Watching them. Smiling at his son. Ashley had to hand it to him. Brayden looked a lot sturdier than she felt.

He'd removed his silver-gray tie. It was dangling from his jacket pocket. And he'd loosened the collar of his white button-down shirt. No more judgelike demeanor. Just a concerned father.

He strolled closer, gave his son a high five and then held a surgical mask over the lower portion of his face when he brushed a kiss on Colton's cheek. "Are you feeling better?"

Colton stuck out his tongue in a *yuck* gesture. "I threw up again."

"It means you're getting well. All the bad junk's leaving your body."

A lie, no doubt. It was probably one of the side effects of the chemo.

Brayden glanced at her. "Are you ready to go?"

No. But Ashley knew she *should* go. The nurse had made it clear that she should keep her visit short because Colton needed his rest. "Sure."

Brayden kissed Colton again. "I've got some things to do," he whispered to his son. "But I'll be back later to tuck you in."

"Uncle Garrett's coming, too?" Colton asked, excitement in his eyes and voice.

"You bet. And I won't tell the doctors if he sneaks you in some candy again."

Colton smiled in that oh-so-secretive way that only a child could manage. "Don't tell 'em Aunt Katelyn did, too."

"Hey, short stuff," Katelyn quipped, looking up from the paperback she held. "Zipped lips, remember? Gummy bears are our little secret."

The moment seemed well past being private. And much too intimate. Ashley murmured a goodbye to Colton, another to Katelyn and headed for the door. However, she barely had time to regain some semblance of composure before Brayden joined her in the hall.

"He's a smart kid," she said, because frankly she had no idea what else to say.

Brayden made a sound of agreement and started up the hall. "He's had a rough time lately. He caught a stomach bug right after chemo. That's why the masks are necessary. His immune system already has enough to deal with."

So did Colton and Brayden.

So did she.

That didn't mean they didn't have to deal with more. And that was something Ashley couldn't put off much longer. Not after what she'd just witnessed.

"Colton's worried that he'll be in the hospital for Christmas," she let Brayden know.

"God, I hope not, but there's always a chance of

that happening. Still, the doctors think he'll be home in a day or two."

Home, but not for good. Probably only until the next round of chemo.

They went through the automatic exit doors and walked outside. The night air was cold. Not a Virginia kind of bitter cold, but it was enough of a chill that Ashley put on her coat and pulled it tightly around her.

As she always did when she stepped into a parking lot or even her own driveway, she looked around. Checking. Making sure no one was lurking. Because even after two and a half years, the fear was still there.

"Could you drop me off at a hotel?" she asked when they approached his car. She checked the time. Almost seven. "I don't want to fly back to Virginia tonight."

He nodded. "I inherited my grandparents' house last year, and even though I still have a lot to renovate, the guest room is finished. You can stay there if you like."

It sounded like an obligatory invitation. And a halfhearted one. Ashley considered letting it pass, but frankly she was tired of this. "Look, Brayden, I think it's time we cleared the air. Don't you?"

He didn't look at her. What else was new? "This isn't easy for either of us."

He made his own sweeping glance around the parking lot, a cop's glance, and opened the car doors so they could get inside. When he started the engine,

Ashley was sure he'd just drive away and ignore the verbal gauntlet she'd tossed.

He didn't.

"When I see you," he said, his words clipped and precise. "I can't help it. I think…"

"Of Dana," she finished. "I know."

"Of that night," he added, getting right to the heart of the matter.

She nodded. Not that he saw her. He had his attention focused on the parking lot. "That night's always with me, too."

The night her sister was killed. Gunned down by an unknown assailant. Except most people suspected that unknown assailant was really Hyatt Chapman.

Ashley's former friend.

Her former client.

Just hours before the shooting she'd helped him get the lightest possible sentence for an aggravated assault charge. Ashley had done that knowing full well that Hyatt was mentally unstable.

Situational ethics, some would say.

Doing her job, others would say.

Either way, she was wrong, and there was nothing she could do to change that. Her sister had paid for her mistake with her life. Though heaven knows, Ashley had tried to undo some of the damage by finding Dana's killer. For two years, seven months and four days, she'd gone over every piece of evidence, every nuance of the case.

Two brothers. Trevor and Hyatt Chapman. They'd grown up with Dana and her. Along with the other player in the saga—Miles Granville—the man that Hyatt and Trevor had allegedly assaulted during a drunken rage because of a business deal gone bad. Miles was also her former boyfriend. Basically, those prior relationships made the case an ethical hornets' nest and one she should never have taken.

And Ashley would regret her decision for the rest of her life.

"You can't forget I withheld evidence about Hyatt Chapman's psychological profile and indirectly allowed Dana to walk into ambush," she reminded him.

"I can't *forgive* it, either. I'm not even sure I've tried. Hell, I'm not sure I *want* to try. And you can't forgive me for putting Dana in a place that made her feel as if she couldn't come to me with the truth."

Yes. Because if Dana had thought Brayden would give Ashley's recently escaped client—Hyatt—a chance to surrender, then Dana might not have gone to that meeting. She might have sent Brayden instead.

And Dana would be alive.

And Brayden and Ashley wouldn't be here having this conversation.

Instead, Dana and he would be trying for another baby. Or perhaps they'd already have one. Either way, Ashley was partly responsible for Dana no longer being alive and that made her partly responsible for

Colton's fate. The only problem with being *partly,* however, was that in this case, it felt overwhelming.

The silence closed in around them, and Ashley blew out a long breath. "Sheez, that was a vanilla argument, considering our past. We spelled out our sins with no gnashing of teeth or yelling. That's a far cry from that night when you told me *I hope like hell I never see your face again.*"

"Yes. A far cry from the night you told me that I'd all but put a bullet in my wife."

Yes. Those were her words all right. Each bitter one of them.

"Far cries aside," she murmured, "you still haven't seen my face."

It was a dare, another gauntlet. And this time, it worked. Brayden lifted his head, turned and nailed his gaze to hers. Unfortunately, his movement came at the same moment when she noticed the car creeping through the parking lot.

Ashley tried to ignore it. Tried and failed. Before she could stop herself, she began to make mental notes of the specifics. A dark green van. Texas plates. Nondescript, except for the fact it had heavily tinted windows. So heavily tinted that she couldn't see the driver.

When it finally crawled by, she pulled her attention away from it and reaimed it at the man who was waiting for her to fulfill her part of the *you still haven't seen my face* dare.

"Want me to run a check on those plates?" Brayden asked.

So, he'd noticed. Of course, he wouldn't have been much of a cop if he hadn't. "No thanks. Old habits, you know."

And those old habits ruled her life. In fact, when Ashley got right down to it, to that elusive bottom line, one of those old habits was the thing that worried her most about becoming pregnant. Giving up her life in Virginia was only part of the problem. Getting past her unresolved issues with Brayden was another. But the *worst* part was facing a fear that so far she'd had zero success in facing.

She cursed herself.

And cursed Brayden, as well.

While she was at it, she cursed the medical community for not having a cure for her nephew.

"You know those scenes in horror movies where the people go into a scary-looking house?" Brayden asked.

Okay. That got her mind off her mental profanity. "Excuse me?"

"Those scenes where people go inside even though they're scared spitless and there's this creepy music playing?"

Now, he looked at her. And she looked at him. Even though the subject was intriguing, and somewhat confusing, Ashley got lost for in moment in those eyes.

Mercy, where had *that* come from?

"Those people are too stupid to live because they ignore all their instincts and do something, well, stupid," he continued. "And the point is, you're not stupid. So, that means I want you to accept my offer to stay in the guest room at my house. You might think I'm a couple of steps below navel lint, but I didn't ask you to come here so you could get hurt."

As one-sided conversations went, that one packed a wallop. Brayden didn't dismiss her fears. Didn't give her one of those icy coplike glances. It was one nearly perfect moment in what had been far from perfect between them.

And in that moment, Ashley knew exactly where this had to go. Maybe she'd always known but had needed this moment, this visit with Colton, for it to sink in. Now, she only hoped she could live with the decision she was about to make.

"I'll do it," she heard herself say.

Brayden nodded. "Good. It won't take us long to get to the house. I've already upgraded the security system, and some officers have volunteered to drive by and keep an eye on the place. It's as safe as I can make it."

He put the car in gear, but she caught his hand to stop him from leaving.

"No, I mean…well, yes, to the guest room," Ashley assured him. "Because you're right—I'm not stupid." Well, not about this anyway. "But yes to helping Colton, too."

His gaze rifled to hers again. But he didn't say a word. He just waited for her to finish.

Ashley did. After she gathered enough breath so she could speak.

"I'll have your baby, Brayden."

Chapter Four

Brayden unlocked his back door, disengaged the security system so he could enter and then immediately reset it once he was inside. What he didn't do was leave the family room. Instead, he stood there a moment in the thick darkness and listened.

If Ashley was still up, she wasn't making a sound.

Of course, it was close to midnight, and after the trip from Virginia, the doctor's appointment, the lab tests and the general stress of the past two days, she was no doubt exhausted. And probably asleep.

Well, hopefully.

Brayden hated to admit it even to himself, but one of the reasons he was so late getting home was that he preferred not to see her. That's why he'd stayed away most of the night before and why he was late again tonight.

And that created a whole new round of guilt for him.

As if he needed more.

He'd asked so much of her, and she'd come

through for Colton. *For him.* Somehow, Ashley had been able to put aside their past to give him the most incredible gift: a chance for his son to get well.

Yet, he wasn't anxious to face her.

That couldn't go on much longer. Eventually, they had to talk. About the insemination. About the upcoming pregnancy. About the logistics of how all of this would work. They had to discuss what would happen once she became pregnant. Would she stay in San Antonio or return to her self-made sanctuary in Virginia?

Brayden refused to change that *once* to an *if.*

Ashley *would* become pregnant.

And the new baby's bone marrow would be a match for Colton. He'd have two healthy children to love and raise.

That was the only scenario he could accept.

He leaned against the wall and listened for several moments but only heard the hum of the fridge in the adjoining kitchen and the rhythmic swings of the pendulum in the grandfather clock. Certain that he could make a clean escape to his bedroom, he crossed the room to the hall.

And came face-to-face with a baseball bat.

He moved out of instinct, latching onto the bat before it could be used to assault him. In the same motion, he grabbed the person's wrist.

His brain registered that it was probably Ashley. *Probably.* But in the back of his mind, there was a concern that it might be an intruder.

"It's me," he managed to say. "It's Brayden."

He heard her then. Definitely Ashley. She made a sound of surprise, of recognition, of relief, but unfortunately her body was a couple of steps ahead of that sound. She'd already started toward him, and it was Brayden who stopped her forward progression.

Ashley rammed into him, off-balancing them both. And they went down to the floor. He managed to turn them at the last possible second so that he took the brunt of the fall. Chivalrous, yes, but not very bright since his head banged the corner of the clock.

Brayden could have sworn he saw stars.

But that wasn't all his chivalrous act had done. No such luck. Ashley landed on top of him. Her breasts against his chest. And their lower bodies aligned in the worst way possible. If it hadn't been for their clothes, they might have had accidental sex.

"It's me," he repeated. Heaven knows why. Ashley obviously knew that by now.

She looked down at him, her breath gusting and hitting him in the face. She smelled like mint toothpaste.

And sex.

Brayden quickly pushed aside that thought. It probably had something to do with the fact that earlier in the evening he'd spent some time in the collection room at the clinic *donating* his contribution for the artificial insemination. Difficult not to think of sex after that.

"I thought it was someone breaking in," she said,

climbing off him. Not easily, either. There was a lot of slippery sliding contact that reminded Brayden he was a man. And that she was a woman.

She rolled to the side, flopped onto her back and lay there, most likely so she could catch her breath. Brayden tried to do the same.

"I didn't hear the garage door open so I didn't think it was you," she explained.

"I figured the garage door would wake you up so I parked in the drive and came in through the back."

More of those gusty breaths punctuated by some mumbling. "I was already awake."

"Obviously." He forced himself to get up and then offered her a hand. Ashley latched onto him, and he helped her to her feet. "Are you hurt?" he asked.

"No. How about you?"

He wouldn't dare mention the stars whirling around his head or the bruise he'd almost certainly have on his butt. "I'll live."

Brayden reached over and turned on the light. A huge mistake. Major. Ashley might not have been sleeping when he arrived, but she was definitely ready for bed.

She wore pajamas. Not some baggy, formless outfit, but Christmas-red silk pj's that clung to just about every inch of her. The top was short. Cropped. And it cropped just enough to expose about an inch or so of her bare stomach.

No bra.

How did he know that?

Because the top was also snug, and he could see the exact shape of her breasts. Small. Firm, from the looks of them. And for reasons Brayden didn't want to explore, he *looked*.

With that look, he felt his body make all kinds of suggestions. Bad suggestions. Suggestions he had no intention of acting on. Brayden forced his attention from her breasts to her face.

Not a great idea, either.

Her hair was tousled, framing her face. Emphasizing that naked mouth and her eyes. It was a reminder that he'd never seen her without her makeup in her pj's.

It didn't seem as if it was something he should be seeing now, either.

"Uh, how was Colton?" Ashley asked, licking her lips. Not a come-on kind of lick either. A fidgety kind of lick. She was nervous.

Welcome to the club.

Brayden was glad she came up with a suitable subject. Because raunchy thoughts aside, he was drawing a blank in the particular area of where they should go from here.

"He's better. He said to tell you hello. Oh, and he also said I should remind you about the snow thing." He paused, shaking his head. "What's that about anyway?"

"He wants snow for Christmas. I told him I'd see

what I could do." She folded her arms over her chest. Which meant she probably knew he'd been gawking at her breasts.

Great. Just great.

In addition to thinking he was naval lint, now she probably thought he was a pervert.

She checked the clock. "Colton was up late, huh? Is that usual for him?"

"It wasn't that late. Not really. I dropped by his room around nine. Tucked him in. Kissed him good-night. And then I had to go to the clinic where the insemination will be done. That's why I'm just now getting home."

That, and the fact that he'd circled the block for the past forty-five minutes.

"Is there a problem at the clinic?" Ashley asked, some alarm in her eyes.

He shook his head. "The doctor met me after hours so I could do some paperwork. Plus, I needed to use the collection room," he added, after clearing his throat.

Brayden saw the moment his meaning registered. "Oh. Got it." She actually blushed, shuffled her feet, licked her lips and generally looked as uncomfortable as he felt. "No news on the tests I took earlier?"

"Nothing yet, but the doctor put a rush on them so we should know something before morning."

"A rush?" she repeated.

"Yes. Because he was concerned that we might

miss your ovulation. Which would mean waiting another month. Anyway, I told the lab to call though as soon as they had results. So, if you hear the phone, that's probably who it'll be. Once we know when you'll be ovulating, then we can schedule the insemination."

Of course, they'd have to verify that she was a suitable candidate for insemination first, but Brayden was hoping they'd get past that hurdle without any problems. That's why he'd gone ahead with the collection so they would be prepared.

Ashley slid her fingers through her hair, ruffling it, and hiking up her top in the process so he could see even more of her stomach. Not that he wanted to see more. When her hair fell back in place, it somehow managed to look even hotter than it had before.

And that was Brayden's cue to head to bed.

If her mussed hair and bare stomach were making him have dirty thoughts, then he didn't need to be in the general vicinity of her.

It was probably just adrenaline or fatigue. Or the fact that his body was on alert because of his trip to the collection room.

"Collection room?" Ashley mumbled under her breath, and Brayden thought maybe he'd said that last part aloud. It gave him a moment of panic. But apparently he'd said aloud no such thing because Ashley didn't looked astonished, only a little queasy.

"Are you all right?" he asked.

"Collection room," she repeated. "Insemination. Sorry, but it all has sort of an ick factor to it."

Okay. That helped with the raunchy thoughts, but it sent his stomach into a tailspin. "You haven't changed your mind about doing this?"

"No. Oh, no. Of course not. It's just..." She made a circular motion with her fingers as if she were trying to figure out how to explain what was on her mind. "The thought of it is a little, well, icky." Another ruffling of her hair. "I'm not making any sense."

"You are. I understand. There's nothing natural about it." And he should know. He was the one who'd been in that collection room.

Even though there was something about this, about Ashley, that felt natural.

Not in a comforting sort of way, either.

Brayden hitched his thumb toward his room, and he almost managed to say a good-night. Almost. But other than the lustful thoughts about her stomach, mouth and hair, he had one other thing on his mind.

"I haven't thanked you—"

"Don't," Ashley interrupted, holding up her hand like a traffic cop. "It only makes me feel guilty."

That was his line, and he was a little surprised to hear it coming from her. "Why does my thanking you make you feel guilty?"

But Brayden immediately winced at the question. Oh, man. Why had he asked that? He hoped this didn't turn into a discussion about Dana.

"Because I keep cursing you for bringing me into this," she explained. "I hate having so many changes, so many uncertainties in my life. And yet I know if our situations were reversed, I would have done the same thing. I would have come to you for help."

It was almost a truce. Except it didn't feel very peaceful. The old issues were still there.

Man, were they ever.

They hadn't forgiven each other. They'd simply put those old issues on hold to do what they had to do.

Since the silence between them quickly became awkward, Brayden was actually thankful when the phone rang. He crossed the room and snatched it up. It was Dr. Underwood, the physician who'd be performing the insemination. When the doctor asked to speak to Ashley, Brayden realized her test results were probably in.

It was time to hold his breath.

Brayden handed her the phone and listened to Ashley's monosyllabic responses.

Yes. Yes. Sure.

What she didn't do was give anything away with her expression. They'd come to that first hurdle, and now he was praying they'd make it across.

"I see," she said to the doctor. "What does that mean exactly?"

Still, her expression revealed nothing.

Okay, so he hadn't intended to play this *what if* game, but her blank expression did it. Brayden

couldn't help but wonder what he was going to do if for some reason Ashley couldn't be inseminated.

She finally said a goodbye, hung up and turned to him. "Everything is okay," she relayed.

Brayden released the breath he'd been holding.

"According to the tests, I'm healthy and shouldn't have any problems conceiving. In fact, I'll be ovulating day after tomorrow."

"That soon." It was great news.

A little overwhelming.

But still great news.

"That soon," she repeated, sounding overwhelmed, as well. "The doctor said I'll need to have the insemination procedure done twice. Once at the onset of ovulation, and then it'll be repeated in twenty-four hours to increase the chances of success."

And success was what this was all about, Brayden reminded himself. Not the thick-as-lead tension simmering between Ashley and him.

"Three more days," she mumbled. "And we'll be finished with the insemination part."

Not much enthusiasm. But he hadn't expected it. "So you'll stay here until then? I mean, I *want* you to stay here until then. Because it'd probably be easier than you flying back and forth to Virginia."

And he was babbling like an idiot.

The corner of her mouth lifted a fraction. "Don't worry, Brayden. I'm as uneasy about this as you are."

Her mouth slid right back into a somber line. "I do have some work that needs to be done on a case, but I can do that via computer, I guess. And then I can be home by the weekend."

Rather than risk more babbling, he just nodded.

More silence. More awkwardness. Until finally Ashley moved. "I'll see you in the morning."

Yes. She would. In fact, they'd be seeing each other for at least three more mornings. And perhaps even some mornings after that if she decided to stay until they had the results of the pregnancy test.

Somehow, he'd have to make himself immune to her choice of sleepwear, or the next three mornings would be hell.

Brayden waited until he heard her close the guest-room door before he went to his own room. The bone-weary fatigue was to the point where he had to get some sleep, or he wouldn't be able to function. He stripped off his shoulder holster, shirt and pants, and then turned on the CD player next to the bed.

He kept the volume low, barely loud enough for him to hear Bruce Springsteen belt out a few lines of "I'm on Fire." Since that was a little too close to music imitating life Brayden reached for the button to skip that particular song.

Car lights swept past his window.

A late-night vehicle wasn't a complete anomaly in his neighborhood since some of the people on the

block did shift work, but the fact that it seemed to be moving so slowly caused Brayden to go to the window. He lifted the curtain a fraction and looked out.

It was a dark van.

Very similar to one that had been in the hospital parking lot earlier that day.

The one that had frightened Ashley.

He drew his weapon. And watched.

Since it was crawling at a snail's pace, Brayden waited until it crossed directly under the streetlight, and he saw the numbers on the license plate. He jotted them down, and without taking his attention off the vehicle, he called headquarters and asked one of the detectives to run the plates.

"Call me back as soon as you have something," Brayden instructed.

He hung up and continued to watch until the van slipped out of sight. Still, Brayden didn't relax. There was something about the vehicle that sent his body on full alert.

His vigilance paid off because several minutes later, he saw the lights again.

It was the same van.

The adrenaline pumped through him. Preparing him, in case there was a fight.

Was this the stalker who'd been after Ashley? He'd taken precautions, yes, but a lot of people had to know she was back in town. It was impossible to keep something like that a secret.

Again, the van cruised out of sight, and Brayden watched until the taillight faded from view. He waited. But it didn't return for a third round.

When the phone rang, he snatched it up so it wouldn't wake Ashley. "It's a rental," the officer relayed. "Registered to a business near the airport."

"By any chance was Hyatt Chapman the person who rented it?" Brayden asked, hoping he was wrong.

Hyatt Chapman, the man who'd escaped from jail the night that Dana was killed. And Hyatt was their prime suspect not only for Dana's murder but also for stalking Ashley.

"No. It's a guy named Jerome Knollings," the officer informed him. "No priors. But nothing else for that matter. He's too clean, if you know what I mean."

Brayden did. It could be an alias. Which meant it could be Hyatt or his brother Trevor.

And that wasn't good.

"Want me to send a unit out to your place?" the officer asked.

"No. Not yet, anyway. Run a thorough check on this Jerome Knollings. I also want to step up surveillance of the neighborhood. If anyone sees this vehicle or any vehicle registered to Knollings in the vicinity, I want it pulled over immediately."

Brayden hung up, knowing his fellow cops would do their best to keep Ashley safe. But he only hoped it was enough. Along with his own precautions, it *had* to be enough.

Because he couldn't fail. Not this time. Not the way he'd failed Dana. He had to keep Ashley safe. Because if he didn't, he'd lose not only her but his son.

Chapter Five

Ashley tapped on his bedroom door. "Brayden?" she softly called out.

Nothing. Well, no vocal response anyway, but she was certain she'd heard him moving around in there.

Since the fax she'd just taken from his machine in the kitchen was marked urgent, she tapped again and then did a full knock. "Brayden?"

Still nothing.

She put her ear to the door, listening for the shower. No sound of running water. But she did hear something. Something she didn't distinguish as footsteps on carpet until it was a second too late.

Brayden jerked open the door while she still had her ear pressed to it.

Ashley dropped back a step and went right into her explanation, or rather that's what she tried to do. However, she got distracted before the first words made it out of her mouth.

Oh, mercy.

Brayden was practically naked. Or maybe it just seemed that way because the naked parts were far more eye-catching than the covered parts. In this case, the *cover* was a pair of loose gray shorts that dipped below his navel. Well below it.

No shirt. In fact, nothing other than those shorts to obstruct her view.

A view she shouldn't be having.

That didn't stop her from looking, though.

All those firm flexing muscles and tan skin. Not a perfect body like some airbrushed model. More interesting than that. From the light sprinkling of bronze-colored chest hair to the faint scar on his left forearm.

Definitely interesting.

In the adjoining sitting room were a treadmill and some weights. Judging from the sweat on his forehead and chest, he'd been working out. Judging from his toned pecs and abs, he worked out often.

And judging from her immediate reaction—the flutter of her pulse, the rushed heartbeat and the warm sensation trickling through her—her own body appreciated the effects.

Since her mouth wouldn't cooperate with an explanation of why she was there, Ashley thrust the fax at him. He looked at her. Not a glance, either. He studied her as if trying to figure out why she'd developed a case of laryngitis.

"Did you manage to get some sleep?" he asked, finally moving his attention to the fax.

"Some."

Still looking at the fax, he crossed the room, picked up a pair of glasses from the nightstand and began reading it. Whatever was on those pages fully captured his attention.

Now, there was another image that did funny things to her body. Brayden looked a little like a studious professor with those glasses and drawn eyebrows, but that studiousness only seemed to emphasize his hot nearly naked body.

Ashley dropped back another step so that no part of her, not even a toe, was in his bedroom.

What was wrong with her anyway?

These feelings were just plain disturbing.

Brayden was her former brother-in-law, for heaven's sake. She'd certainly never had these sort of thoughts about him when Dana was alive. She'd noticed he was good-looking, of course. She would have had to be blind not to notice that. But she'd never lusted after him.

Until now, that is.

And there was no mistake about it.

She was definitely lusting after him.

With his attention still on the fax, he sank down onto the edge of the bed and idly brushed his hand through his hair. Then he reached for the phone and punched in some numbers.

"Lt. O'Malley," he said to whomever answered. "I want a situation report and follow-up on this fax."

Okay, that was a way to get her mind off lustful thoughts. Because situation reports and follow-ups sounded urgent. Ashley prayed it didn't have anything to do with Colton or the insemination procedure.

"I have to go into headquarters," Brayden said to her when he hung up the phone. "I'll have my sister come over and stay with you."

His sister the cop. Ashley nodded and did some thinking.

Brayden slipped off his glasses, tossed them back onto the nightstand and tipped his head to the computer. "If you need to e-mail anyone or do some work while I'm gone, you can use that. It's got a firewall and some modifications so it's secure. It's the same for the phone."

Ashley mumbled a thanks. What she didn't do was leave, even though it was obvious he'd need to take a shower since he intended to go into work.

"I wouldn't mind checking on my house while I'm here in town," she said. Not because that was what was on her mind, but because she wanted to feel him out so she would know what was bothering him. "Maybe I can drive over later?"

"Wait until I can go with you." The words were not exactly a request. "We can swing by there tomorrow on the way to the clinic for the insemination."

Okay. That did it. She wanted security, yes, because she wasn't stupid. But she also wanted the truth. "Does that fax and your need to go into work

have something to do with the van that drove past your house twice last night?"

He flexed his eyebrows. "I was hoping you hadn't noticed it."

"I noticed. So, what's the verdict?"

He glanced back through the fax again, even though Ashley was willing to bet he had already committed the pertinent details to memory. "It's not the same van that was in the parking lot at the hospital. That one was green. This one is midnight-blue, and this one was leased to a guy named Jerome Knollings."

Not Hyatt. Or his brother Trevor. Thank heaven. But that didn't exactly cause Ashley to breathe easier. Because she knew, she just knew, that all was not well. "Knollings is an alias?"

He nodded, eventually.

That sent her hands onto her hips. "This feels a little like déjà vu, Brayden. Like those days when I used to cross-examine you in court and you'd give as little info as possible until I dragged it out of you."

"There's not a lot of info to give. This guy might have nothing to do with you. There are at least a dozen reasons why someone would assume an alias."

"Like my reason, for instance?"

Another nod, followed by a slight scowl. "Like yours. But there are a couple of other scenarios that could be playing out here. There's a woman who lives up the street who recently took out a restraining order against her ex-husband. Could be this Knol-

lings is after her. Or it could be just someone canvassing the neighborhood for burglaries. That kind of stuff happens all the time."

Yes, it did. But it wasn't those particular scenarios that warranted his cop-sister staying at the house while Brayden was at headquarters. After all, there were already patrol cars driving by practically every half hour. And then there was his security system. Far better than the one she had in Virginia. Yet, Brayden still thought his sister's presence might be necessary.

Why?

"Look, this Knollings guy might be legit," Brayden continued. "He might have nothing at all to do with you. *Nothing.* Cruising down streets at midnight wasn't your stalker's MO. He was a caller, a letter writer. That kind of sicko likes to keep some physical distance between him and his target. That's not what Knollings was doing."

True. But that didn't mean her stalker hadn't changed his preferred method of operation. And that gave Ashley a whole new set of concerns.

Huge concerns.

If the stalker was back, and if he began his old games of torment and threats, would he limit those threats to her? Or would he turn his attention to Brayden since she was staying at his house?

Or worse.

Would he go after Colton?

That caused Ashley's heart to race for a whole different reason.

"You have someone staying at the hospital with Colton, right?" she asked.

"Of course. My dad's with him right now, and Mom will be there this afternoon. They're both former cops. So, let's not borrow trouble, okay?"

Well, that was one thing they could agree on.

Because Ashley was certain they already had enough trouble without borrowing more.

Chapter Six

It was like walking into a time capsule.

The foyer and the adjoining living room of her house were exactly as Ashley had left them two and a half years ago. Not a piece of furniture was out of place. Right down to the magazines and somewhat gaudy art deco coasters she'd left on the polished limestone coffee table.

Ashley trailed her fingers over the umbrella stand in the entry and strolled through the dining room and into the kitchen. The property manager she'd hired had done a good job. No dust. Everything was clean. Everything in place. Well, everything except for the phone that had been ripped from the wall. The one that now lay neatly on the countertop near her espresso maker.

She'd done that herself.

Not the *laying neatly* part, but the ripping part, and the memory of it was as fresh as if it had happened hours and not years ago. The stalker had made one

call too many that night, and she'd snapped. She'd taken out her fears and frustrations on the silver-gray phone that matched her slate countertops.

The fit of temper hadn't helped. It had only been the final straw that had sent her on the run.

Brayden stayed back in the tile-framed arched doorway that separated the kitchen from the dining room. Probably because he could tell she needed a moment alone. A moment Ashley hadn't even known she needed until she'd felt the pressure in her chest.

Mercy, she had once loved this place.

Her *home*.

To buy it, she's spent a huge chunk of the money she'd inherited years earlier when both her parents were killed in a car accident. And then, she'd shelled out even more money to begin decorating and landscaping it.

For all the good it'd done.

She'd been over halfway through creating her own personal version of paradise, only to allow herself to be driven from it by a man too cowardly to show his face.

That riled her—now.

It was ironic that she was now probably strong enough to face him, and she couldn't. Because it was no longer about her. It was also about Colton and the baby she needed to have to save his life.

"It's starting to sleet," Brayden let her know.

Ashley glanced out the wide glass doors that led

to the patio. The icy drizzle was dimpling the surface of the lagoon-blue pool, and the thick gray clouds predicted that it wouldn't let up before nightfall.

Not good.

It'd mean the roads would probably ice over. Not a complete rarity in San Antonio, but it would create far from normal driving conditions.

"We should leave soon," Brayden added. "To give us a little extra time to get to the clinic."

"You're right," she said picking up the ripped-out phone from the counter. Ashley tried to fit it back onto the metal slot still attached to the wall. She struggled with it a few moments before she heard Brayden walk across the floor toward her.

Meeting her gaze for a moment, he calmly took the phone from her and slid it back in place. "Nervous about the procedure?" he asked.

She was nervous about a lot of things, but instead of vocalizing that, Ashley nodded. And then she vocalized something that she wished she'd kept to herself. "I hope you have strong sperm."

He made a sound—a single burst of semilaughter that stayed deep within his throat.

Ashley shook her head. "I meant—"

"I know what you meant. The doctor said the insemination wouldn't be painful," he continued, looking a little flustered at the turn in the conversation.

Ashley knew how he felt. She'd been flustered since he'd appeared on her porch in Virginia, and

there wasn't a chance the frustration would lessen anytime soon. In fact, she was betting it would get a lot worse.

"I can go in the procedure room with you," he offered. "If you want…"

"This is really a solo kind of thing."

He nodded. Some relief joined the discomfort in his expression.

"There's so much to think about, you know?" she asked. It was rhetorical.

Of course, he knew.

He answered anyway. Well, sort of. He voiced one of the repeated concerns that kept going through her head. "Having a baby's a big step in anyone's life."

Yes. And for her, that step was huge. "I always figured I'd have a child. Someday. Eventually." Because she needed something to do with her suddenly fidgety hands, Ashley checked out the fridge. Nothing, with the exception of a yellow box of baking soda. "I just didn't think that child would be the result of insemination."

Brayden nodded. "Because of that ick factor?"

That, and she'd just figured a pregnancy would happen under more normal circumstances.

Or at least pleasurable ones.

Hopefully, Brayden had had an easier time providing his contribution in the collection room than she'd have receiving it. Of course, there wasn't anything about this situation that could be construed as *easy*. One way or another, this would change everything.

"I'll love this baby," she assured him. "It won't be just about providing a sibling donor for Colton." But it didn't sound like so much an assurance as it did an attempt to convince herself.

Which it wasn't.

There were a lot of blurs and uncertainties about all of this, but her feelings for this yet-to-be-conceived child wasn't one of them. If Brayden and she succeeded in making a baby, their child would definitely be loved.

His phone rang, and Brayden slipped it from his belt. "Lt. O'Malley," he answered.

Rather than eavesdrop, Ashley walked past him and went through the hall so she could make a quick check of her bedroom. Like the rest of the house, it was in perfect order. The bed made. The carpet vacuumed. Nothing seemed out of place. Until her gaze fell on the answering machine next to her bed.

The tiny red bead of light was frantically pulsing.

Her heart started to pulse with it.

She went closer, but not too close. Ashley eyed the machine as if it were a poisonous snake ready to strike. In a way, it was. She was almost afraid to press the button that would play the message someone had left for her.

And that brought her to another thought.

She'd had the phone disconnected two and a half years ago, so there should have been no messages. That light shouldn't have been blinking.

Since her heart seemed ready to beat out of her chest, she forced herself to calm down and consider something, anything, less sinister than what she'd already considered. Maybe the property manager had reconnected the phone for her? Maybe Brayden had, since he knew they'd be dropping by tonight?

But Ashley didn't think either of those things had happened.

She reached out, her index finger hovering over the button that would play the recorded message. However, she stopped when she heard the hurried footsteps behind her.

Just like that, her heart sprang to her throat. Her muscles tightened. Her body braced itself for the fight. Oh, mercy. Had the stalker found her and broken in?

Ashley whirled around.

And saw Brayden.

Just Brayden.

No stalker. No bogeyman. No threat that her body was preparing itself to see. Almost immediately, she felt herself relax.

Until she saw the look on his face.

"What's wrong?" she asked.

He didn't answer right away and that caused the fight-or-flight adrenaline to return in full force.

"The clinic caught fire," he told her.

A dozen thoughts went through Ashley's head. None good. "How? When?"

"About a half hour ago."

She touched her fingertips to her lips. "Was it arson?"

"Maybe. They're still trying to put out the blaze so it might be a while before we know for sure."

"What about the doctor—"

"He was injured," Brayden said, confirming her fears. "Not seriously, but it was bad enough that he's on his way to the hospital via ambulance."

Oh, God.

This couldn't be happening. It just couldn't be. But it was. Heaven help them, it was.

Brayden paused. "There's more."

Ashley wasn't sure she could deal with more, but she braced herself.

"The semen they were going to use for the insemination was destroyed."

That did it. Her legs gave way, and she sat down on the bed. All their carefully laid plans were gone. *Gone.*

Worse, Ashley knew in her heart this wasn't an accident.

Someone was intentionally trying to stop them from saving Colton. Or rather someone was trying to stop *her.*

And she was positive that someone was the stalker.

BECAUSE HE HAD TO DO something, *anything,* Brayden phoned headquarters. Not for an update—he'd

just received one. But to demand a thorough investigation of the fire. It was an unnecessary demand since he knew the arson detectives would do their jobs and that they would be thorough. If it was indeed arson, they'd likely find evidence of it.

For all the good it'd do Colton.

The doctor was hurt. The clinic damaged. And his vials of semen destroyed.

Hell.

Brayden leaned his back against the wall and slid to the floor so he could sit down.

Ashley buried her face in her hands. "Please don't tell me you think this was a coincidence or an accident?"

He didn't.

But Brayden kept his speculation to himself.

Besides, there was nothing he could do about the fire now. Nothing. He could only try to deal with the aftermath.

And the aftermath, he soon realized, would be a bitch.

Several possible solutions came to mind, including really bad ones, but he nixed one in particular right off the bat.

"Most clinics will already be closed," Brayden mumbled, taking out the phone that he'd just put away. "We had the last appointment on the schedule. But I'll call around and see if we can find someone at the hospital who'll do it."

Because he was watching her, he saw Ashley ease her hands down from her face. "And what will you ask for? An emergency artificial insemination?"

It sounded even worse than he'd imagined it would, and Brayden had imagined that it would sound pretty bad. "If I have to. I don't want to wait another month. Colton might need that month."

"Exactly." With that emphatic one-word agreement, she got to her feet. "But think this through, Brayden. The weather's terrible. There will be accidents. Emergency rooms all over the city will be packed. No doctor is going to give us priority for an insemination."

That didn't stop him.

Nothing would.

He got up, as well, stormed across the room and grabbed the phone book tucked on the bottom shelf of her nightstand. He riffled through it, found the listings for hospitals and ripped them out. He did the same for physicians and passed Ashley a handful of the pages.

"I hope you have your cell phone because I need you to start calling. I'll do the same. But first I want to make sure your security system is working."

She pulled back her shoulders, and something went through her eyes. Alarm, definitely. Maybe something more. But Brayden didn't have time to ask her what exactly. They already had enough *alarm* to deal with.

Ashley glanced down at the phone next to her bed, peeled off her coat and tossed the garment on top of the covers. "The controls for the security system are in the laundry room."

That shedding of her coat must have been a sign of her bolstered resolve because Ashley no longer looked hesitant or argumentative. She led him back through the house and along the way she grabbed her phone from her purse that she'd left in the foyer.

Brayden made his first call, to his family doctor, while Ashley opened the security control panel mounted on the laundry-room wall. By the time he'd set the sensors to cover all areas, including the windows and garage, he'd gotten yet more bad news. His doctor was out of town for the holidays.

Brayden cursed.

This just wasn't his night.

Ashley didn't fare any better. Her call to her former doctor was redirected to a voice mail, and she left a message. She tried again with the next number on the page.

Brayden did the same. His call was to an emergency room, where he had to explain—not easily—what he wanted to three different people. Each insisted it'd be a long wait for a nonemergency procedure and that it would require several layers of authorization.

Ashley huffed and clicked off her phone. "I'm just going to say this because I figure we're both thinking it anyway." She didn't continue until his gaze came to hers. "There's a faster way to do this."

Yes.

It was a way his body had already suggested.

And it wasn't going to happen.

Brayden ran his finger down the page to find the next number, but Ashley snatched the pages from him.

"Think this through, Brayden. It's Saturday night. Most clinics are already closed. And even if we find a clinic or a hospital and manage not to get into an accident while we're driving there, you'll still have to make another trip to the *collection room*."

"So?"

"So, there'll be paperwork and probably even more lab tests because they'll need to do some cover-their-butt precautions to protect themselves from a potential lawsuit. We'll be darn lucky if all of this happens before morning. By then, we've missed hours. Crucial hours that could mean the difference between a baby or no baby. I hate to be crude, or insulting to you, but we can get this done in fifteen minutes. Maybe less."

He had no idea how to answer that. *None.* She was right. That much he did know. They could get it done faster the old-fashioned way.

But at what cost?

Oh, man.

At an enormous cost no doubt.

And could he even do it?

Brayden had never questioned his ability to have sex, but this was way out of his realm of normal experience. Besides, it was Ashley. He couldn't—

"We could think of it as clinical sex," she added.

As if that would help.

Even clinical sex required him to become fully aroused. It required him to feel a basic lustful attraction to her.

Which he was sorry to say, he felt.

"Mercy," she mumbled, adding a few choice words of profanity after it. Ashley tossed her phone and the pages onto the nearby dryer.

She didn't stop there.

Mumbling something indistinguishable under her breath, she shoved up her oatmeal-colored sweater so she could reach the side zipper on her pants. Her movements and her mumblings were jerky and awkward.

"If it helps—don't even think of it as sex," she continued, her words rushed. Almost frantic.

Ashley kicked her shoes aside, one of them smacking against the wall, and she let her unzipped pants slide to the floor. She stepped out of them and then proceeded to peel off her pantyhose. "In fact, don't think about it at all. Think of nothing. Absolutely nothing. Just react like any man would react to being offered sex."

Brayden shook his head. Why, he didn't know. He damn sure wasn't declining her offer.

Because he knew what he had to do.

Huffing again, Ashley reached behind him, her body whispering against his, and she slapped off the light. It didn't plunge them into total darkness

though, as she'd probably hoped. As *he* had hoped. The security lights in the backyard filtered through the thick watery blocks of glass, making it seem as if they were surrounded by shimmering candlelight.

"Don't think about it," Ashley repeated.

She reached out, ran her fingers down his arm. Rubbed softly, despite the fact her hand was trembling.

Brayden caught her trembling wrist to stop her from touching him. In the pale flickering light, their gazes collided. Held.

Neither of them looked away.

Neither moved.

The only sounds were their rushed breaths and the sleet spitting against the glass.

She stood there, bare legged. Waiting. And looking far better than he wanted her to look.

He didn't want her.

He didn't want this.

But he wanted his son to live.

And that was what he focused on.

Cursing fate, Brayden let go of the grip he had on her hand so he could pull her slightly closer to him. Not exactly a loving, intimate act, either. It was simply to establish the contact he needed to have sex with her.

Ashley went right into his arms as if she belonged there.

Funny that he'd think of that because *belonging there* was exactly how it felt. She fit. They fit. As if

they'd been made for each other. Her body against his. Her face in the curve of his neck. Her bare right leg wedged between his.

Brayden pushed all those *fit* comparisons aside.

It was sex.

Just sex.

That's all it ever could be.

"Here?" she asked.

He briefly considered taking her back to the bedroom but decided against it. It would just waste time. Time where he'd be wrestling with the guilt he was already feeling. And he probably wasn't the only one. Ashley was no doubt dealing with her own demons.

"Here," he confirmed.

There were no kisses. No lovers' caresses. No foreplay. He curved his arm around her waist and hauled her tighter against him. To him. Until they were pressed against each other for only one purpose.

"What do you need me to do?" she whispered.

Brayden was positive she wasn't asking about fundamentals here. Ashley undoubtedly wanted to know what got him hot. But it was an unnecessary concern on her part. Just the feel of her in his arms was enough.

Hell.

It was enough.

He felt the blood rush through his head. And to other parts of him. The heat slammed through his body. That kick. That overwhelming rush of need. To mate.

To take.

Brayden didn't even try to slow things down because this wasn't a moment to savor. This wasn't about making love. It was sex. He only hoped he could remember that.

He lifted her off the floor, and since the washer was close that's where he put her. He didn't waste any time. He stripped off her panties. A swatch of black silk and lace. He unzipped his pants, freed himself from his boxers and moved between her legs.

He slowed only long enough to slip his fingers past her pubic hair to make sure she was ready. She was.

Somehow.

He didn't want think about *why* she was ready. In fact, he went with Ashley's advice and didn't think at all. That bit of wisdom just might get him through this.

Latching onto her hips to position her, Brayden positioned himself, as well. So that the slick heat of her body brushed against his erection. Another slam of need. It created a raw aching demand to take her.

So, that's what he did.

Brayden pushed into her and tried to ignore the soft feminine sound she made. A rich moan that came from deep within her throat. He tried to ignore her scent. Tried to ignore the way she took him into her body.

All of him.

Every inch of him.

Until her firm muscles gripped him. And gave him exactly what he needed.

Ashley wrapped her legs around his waist and rocked against him. Moving with him. Slowly at first. Then faster. Much faster. Matching his strokes, shoving her body against his until they found a frantic necessary rhythm.

Now, his body demanded.

Take her now.

So that's what he did. Brayden continued to push into her. Hard. Stroke after stroke. Thrusting into that heat and moisture.

The need to take her rose, surged, propelled him to another place. To a place where guilt and feelings slipped away, where instincts and primal needs seized control of every part of him. That primal need drove him. Consumed him. So that he pushed deeper.

Harder.

Faster.

Until that one word pounded in his head. Pounded in cadence with own heartbeat. With his breath. With hers. Pounded with each thrust.

Now.

Until it pounded through his entire body. Until it became his only thought. His only…everything.

Now.

Now.

Now.

Brayden gathered Ashley close and did exactly what he needed to do. He gave in to that demand for *now.*

And he surrendered.

Chapter Seven

Ashley figured if she looked up the word *awkward* in the dictionary, there'd be a picture of her dressing in the laundry room while Brayden zipped his pants.

Not that she was watching him do that, of course. He wasn't watching her, either. In fact, they were doing everything humanly possible not to look at each other. However, she heard the rasp of the metal from his zipper, the metaphorical punctuation mark, for what had just happened.

Out of the corner of her eye, she saw him move to the doorway. With his back to her. He bracketed his hands on the jamb and waited.

Ashley hurried, locating her panties and pants on the floor. She pulled them both on.

"The doctor told me I'm supposed to lie down for twenty minutes or so," she let him know.

Not easily. But she got out the words without stuttering. She wouldn't mention the part about elevating her hips. It seemed too personal. Ironic, since they'd just had some very personal contact.

Which Brayden had somehow managed to keep impersonal.

Well, what had she expected? Brayden had done exactly as she'd asked him to do. He hadn't thought about it. He'd simply done what was required of him as the male contributor in this baby-making venture.

He glanced over his shoulder at her. The briefest glance possible. Then he turned, and, without saying a word, he scooped her up in his arms. It was definitely not a romantic gesture, though. It was a simple follow-up procedure to minimize the effects of gravity and thereby improve their chances of a conception.

Brayden took her up the hall to her bedroom and laid her on the bed. Gently. Carefully. As if she might break. He stepped away and went to the window. Ashley waited until she was sure he wasn't looking at her before she slid a pillow beneath the backs of her thighs.

"Do you need anything?" he asked. "Is there something I can get you?"

"I'm okay," she lied.

Ashley didn't have to see Brayden's face to know what he was feeling. She could hear it in the stoic undertones of his voice.

He felt guilty.

An emotion she totally understood. She felt guilty, too. Seriously guilty. And she hadn't even had an orgasm.

In fact, she'd worked hard *not* to have one.

Probably one for the record. But then, she'd experienced a lot of firsts tonight.

And to think, they were supposed to repeat this *procedure* in twenty-four hours. A way of further increasing their chances of success. With the clinic damaged and the doctor injured, did that mean Brayden and she would have to have sex the old-fashioned way again?

Perhaps.

Twenty-four hours wasn't a lot of time to put something like this together. No. It would be faster for them to just, well, do it.

She felt her pulse flutter in her throat.

Oh, mercy.

Ashley firmly reminded her pulse that none of this was for fun. This was for procreation purposes only. And in only six days they might know one way or another if their procreation attempt had succeeded.

Of course, she'd be back in Virginia when she got the verdict on that. She had already purchased the airline tickets and confirmed the flight. Day after tomorrow, she'd be out of there and would already be trying to put her life back in order.

Temporarily anyway.

That order would have to shift no matter what the results of the pregnancy test. If it was negative, Brayden and she would have to go through this all over again. For heaven knows how long. It could take

months. And if the test was positive. Well, that would take months of shifting and adjusting, as well.

Brayden lifted his hands slightly, palms up, but immediately drew them back down. "I feel as if I should say I'm sorry."

"For what?" Ashley asked, not sure she really wanted to hear this.

"I was rough. I'm not usually rough." He didn't end that comment the way a comment would normally end. There was a questioning inflection.

"You didn't hurt me—if that's what you're concerned about."

Sheez.

She wanted to hit herself. Why had she just given him carte blanche to discuss this? It was obvious Brayden didn't want to talk about it. She didn't want to talk about it, either.

And she was almost certain she believed that.

"It was sex, *clinical sex,* as you put it," he said slowly as if he were carefully choosing his words, which he no doubt was. This conversation was like clog dancing through a minefield. "But I could have...I mean, for you, I should have—"

"I didn't expect you to," Ashley interrupted.

Even though he almost had.

And probably would have.

If she hadn't held back. Thank goodness for guilt. It'd served her well tonight.

Brayden glanced at her. A puzzling glance,

maybe? Hopefully not a puzzling glance. Okay, she should have just kept quiet.

"Open mouth, insert foot," Ashley mumbled under her breath. Maybe he wasn't talking about her orgasm—or the lack of—after all. Maybe he'd meant something else, and by her addressing it, it opened the subject for discussion.

Great. Just great.

"Still," Brayden commented. And that was all he said for several moments. "I should have...well, I just should have."

So, he *had* been talking about an orgasm. "Don't worry about it. We were both in that whole speed-counts mode."

She hoped that would let him off the hook so he'd drop the subject.

He didn't.

"It just feels as if I used you. I *did* use you." No slow, calculated speech that time. The words just rushed out. "And I don't like feeling like this, Ashley. I don't like doing what we had to do."

Okay. That clarified things. In addition to his obvious overwhelming guilt, sex with her hadn't even been marginally enjoyable. But that made sense, of course.

It couldn't have been enjoyable.

Because if it had been, then it would have been like betraying Dana.

Ashley was thankful that Brayden's phone rang

and even more thankful when he stepped out in the hall to take the call. It not only put an end to the excruciating conversation, it also gave her some much-needed time alone.

Figuring she'd met her timed elevation requirement, Ashley got up from the bed and went to the adjoining bathroom so she could freshen up. Except one glance in the mirror, and she realized she didn't look as if she needed much freshening. Heck, her makeup wasn't even mussed.

The only thing in disarray was her heart.

Oh, and her nerves.

Definitely those.

She felt raw. That feeling didn't improve when she glanced in the mirror again and saw the reflection of something on the edge of the claw-footed tub.

A blood-red candle.

Clutching her hand to her chest, Ashley whirled around, her gaze slashing to each corner of the room. To make sure no one else was in there. To make sure she was indeed alone.

No one was in the corners, but that left the tub. Specifically what might be *in* the tub, behind the opaque shower curtain that completely encircled it.

Why would the cleaning crew have left out a candle?

And for that matter, why shut the shower curtain?

No one had used that tub or shower in well over two years.

She stilled. And listened for any small sound that would confirm or deny her worst suspicions. And that was *worst* in just about every sense of the word. Because if this was the stalker, the person who'd killed Dana, then not only was she in danger, but Brayden was, as well.

Ashley almost called out for him. But she forced herself to think. Maybe it was just a candle. And it wasn't unusual for her to burn them while she was bathing. In fact, it was common. She could have left one there, and maybe the maid had thought it was decoration. That would explain why it hadn't been moved for cleaning.

"Just a candle," Ashley repeated.

But that didn't mean she wasn't going to take precautions. While keeping her attention nailed to the shower curtain, she reached beneath the sink, trying not to make a sound, and she fumbled around until she located a plunger. Not an ideal weapon, but one bit of movement, one shadow, one thing out of place, and she'd use it as a weapon.

She reached out, latched onto the curtain and gave it a hard jerk to the left. The metal hooks rattled and the sheet of silky cloth slithered around the circular bar that supported it.

No stalker.

It took Ashley a moment just to catch her breath, but the breath was short-lived. Because while the tub didn't hold a stalker, it wasn't empty.

Inside the tub, sitting on the pale ivory porcelain was yet another candle. Tipped over. Soot covered the wick as if it'd been recently lit. And next to it was a carefully arranged bouquet of dried flowers.

Like the flowers that had caught fire at her rental house in Virginia.

Gasping, Ashley jumped back. She banged into the sink and knocked off a porcelain toothbrush holder in the process. It crashed to the tile floor, shattering, and the noise echoed through the room.

Brayden's racing footsteps quickly followed that noise. Within seconds, he rounded the corner. "Are you all right?"

Ashley didn't answer him. Instead, she pointed to the candle and the dried flowers.

He pushed past her. Actually placing himself between the tub and her, he examined what had sent her heart into a tailspin.

"You didn't leave that?" he asked.

She shook her head. "No."

"Don't panic. It could be nothing. I'll have them checked for prints. Hell, I'll have the whole place checked. First, though, I'm getting you out of here. We'll go back to my house and I'll call in some officers."

He took out his phone, presumably to arrange for that, when Ashley remembered her own phone. The one next to her bed. How in the name of heaven had she forgotten about that?

Avoiding the shards of porcelain, she stepped around him, made a beeline for the nightstand and picked her coat up off of the phone. The light was still on.

Still blinking.

She was aware of Brayden moving behind her. Of him watching her. Pulling in her breath, Ashley reached out and pressed the "play message" button on her answering machine.

"You have one message," the perky female mechanical voice announced.

There was a slight jolt of static. Followed by yet another voice.

Not mechanical, perky, or female.

But it did have an artificial sound to it, as if it'd been recorded and then spliced together to form the sentence.

Four words. Four simple words that made her feel as if someone had put a knife to her throat.

"Welcome home, Ashley Palmer."

Chapter Eight

"What do you mean the 'Welcome home, Ashley Palmer' message could have been *legit?*" Ashley asked him. "My phone shouldn't even have been on, so there's no way I should have had a message, legit or otherwise."

Brayden mentally went through the explanation he'd received just minutes earlier from the lead detective. He hoped the explanation made sense when he repeated it to Ashley.

"The manager of the company who oversees your property said the phone reconnection was a mistake. A clerical error. He thinks what happened was one of his employees was supposed to do a work order for another residence, and this employee went to your address instead."

Ashley sat on the living-room sofa and curled her sock-covered feet beneath her. "A mistake," she repeated, not sounding at all sure she believed that.

Brayden was right there with her, on the same

doubting page, and he was still trying to decide if the manager's explanation fit the evidence.

She grabbed a throw pillow and hugged it to her chest, practically putting it in a choke hold. "That might explain the phone being on, but what about the message itself?"

"The manager said they routinely send automated welcome home messages to their clients who've been out of town. A way of letting the client know they care."

Ashley paused a couple of seconds, probably to consider that. "So, it wasn't a threat after all." That choke hold on the pillow eased up a bit. Temporarily. "Except it still feels like one."

Yes. It did.

His instincts told him not to back off from his concerns just yet. But Brayden was wondering if he could even trust his instincts where Ashley was concerned.

The boundaries between him and Ashley were definitely blurring.

Which probably had something to do with the fact that he'd had sex with her only hours earlier. Hard to get around that new wrinkle in their relationship.

She looked up at him, her eyes slightly narrowed. "What about the candle and the flowers? Did the manager have an explanation for those, too?"

Brayden shrugged. "Only that the cleaning crew could have put the items in the bathtub and forgot to take them back out."

On the surface it was a tidy explanation.

He hated tidy explanations.

However, Brayden kept that to himself. Ashley already had enough to deal with without adding his suspicions.

She gave that pillow a punch, a hard one, tossed it back in the corner of the sofa and jammed her hands in her hair. "Okay. Sounds reasonable," she mumbled. "But it sure didn't feel *reasonable* when I was in that bathroom."

Brayden made a sound of agreement and might have added more if he hadn't noticed the bruise on her left wrist. A distinctive thumb-print-sized bruise that had already started to turn purple. One he'd no doubt given her. Despite her denial, he had been too rough.

Hell.

Was there anything about this frickin' night that had gone right?

His body immediately offered him an answer.

An answer that Brayden disregarded.

While he was at it, he disregarded the slight buzz of pleasure that was still with him. The buzz that always came with release, with sex.

A buzz he hadn't felt in a long, long time.

"All of those coincidences could have happened," she continued, still mumbling. "Right?"

Brayden nodded, his affirmation setting off that BS meter in his head. And he was glad it did. Despite its implications, concentrating on the manager's BS

explanation was a welcome alternative to the other things on his mind.

He got up and turned away from her so he wouldn't have to look at that bruise. Or at her. Maybe putting her out of sight would cause that buzz to stop buzzing, as well. "I'm still having a team go through your house, just to make sure everything's okay."

"Thanks." A few moments later, she groaned. "I feel so stupid. Next time I have a bout of paranoia, I'll try not to involve the police."

He considered several comebacks but decided against voicing any of them. It seemed a good time for another nod so that's what he did, especially since he wasn't convinced it was paranoia.

He hated coincidences almost as much as he hated tidy explanations.

His cell phone rang, and when he saw the number on the display screen, he stepped out of the living room to take the call. This probably wasn't anything Ashley needed to hear, not after the night she'd already had.

"It's me," his brother, Garrett, said after Brayden answered. "You wanted me to check on Colton. I did, and he's fine. Joe's with him tonight."

That made Brayden breathe a little easier. His brother-in-law, Joe Rico, was one tough cop. He trusted Joe to do everything humanly possible to protect his son.

If protection was necessary, that is.

"Is the evidence response team at Ashley's house?" Brayden asked.

Even though Brayden tried to keep his voice low, at the sound of her name, Ashley looked up, automatically snaring his gaze. She was still on the sofa and had turned on the TV, pretending to watch the late-night news. But he knew for a fact it was a pretense.

She was pale. Too pale. And despite her apparent willingness to accept the manager's explanation about the flowers, candle and greeting, that willingness didn't seem genuine.

"The team's at her house now," Garrett informed him. "But they've found nothing so far. There are prints, of course, but they belong to Ashley, her cleaning lady—and you."

Prints. Somehow he'd forgotten his prints would be there. "You'll probably find mine in several rooms."

Especially the laundry room.

Because that buzz rippled through him again, Brayden let that thought and the accompanying images slide right on by. Well, he tried to anyway. But some of the thoughts stayed with him a couple of seconds. Specifically the image of Ashley's body. For some reason, the memory of that just wouldn't go away.

This time, the feeling was more than a buzz. The muscles in his lower body clenched. An aftershock of pleasure. Brayden curled his hand into a fist and pressed it hard to his forehead. Much more of this and he'd need a cold shower.

"Are you still there?" Garrett asked.

"Yeah." And he had to get his mind back on the conversation because his brother was apparently waiting for an explanation about those prints. "Ashley and I stopped by her house on the way to the clinic. She wanted to check on the place."

"Good thing you were at her house and not the clinic. I heard about the fire. Suspected arson, huh? You think it's tied to you and Ashley?"

"Maybe. And maybe it was just bad luck, for the doctor and for us. By the way, how's Dr. Underwood?"

"He's still in the hospital with burns to his hands. I don't think he'll be at work anytime soon. How does that affect your plans? Does this mean you missed your chance to make a baby this month?"

Brayden debated how much he should say but knew sooner or later his family would have to know. "Not exactly. Ashley and I took care of it."

And he left it at that.

Garrett paused. For a long time. "Oh."

That *oh* conveyed a lot. Brayden knew what Garrett was thinking.

"Oh?" Garrett repeated, fishing for more.

"Yes, oh!" Brayden snapped.

"Sorry. If you think it'll help, I'll come over and pick a fight with you. Might burn off some of that anger."

"It won't help." Nothing would. Not even that cold shower he'd threatened his body with. "And I'd

prefer you didn't say anything else about it. Not to anyone. Not to me. *Especially* not to me."

"I live to serve and please," Garrett said, sarcasm dripping from his voice. But the sarcasm faded when he continued. "I'm sorry. Being with Ashley couldn't have been easy for either of you."

"It wasn't."

And it was past time they moved on to a different subject. Since his brother probably wouldn't move them in that new direction, Brayden took the initiative. "I need you to work with Katelyn and Joe to make sure Colton's being watched at all times. I also want patrols stepped up at the hospital and at my place. Just in case."

Another of those pauses, as if Garrett were about to call him on the abrupt switch in topic. But his brother obviously knew it wouldn't do any good. "Anything else?"

"I need some files. Those for the investigation into Ashley's stalker. And the ones for Dana's murder."

"Brayden." Garrett doled out some profanity. "You don't need to be going back through all of that—"

"It's exactly what I need to be doing. You and I both know what happened to Dana could be related to Ashley's stalker."

"*Could be.* Those are the operative words. And even if they are related, you shouldn't be the one trying to connect the dots. Hear that? You're too close to both victims, Brayden. Hell, you're trying to get one of them pregnant."

A reminder he didn't need.

"Just please get me the files, Garrett. If there are any dots to be connected, I want to find them."

The *please* was deceptive because it wasn't a request. He hated to pull rank, on his own brother no less, but one way or another he would go back over that information. That *tidy explanation* was already starting to gnaw away at him.

"Is that it?" Garrett asked, obviously riled.

"Yes." Brayden was about to hang up when he thought of something else. "What about that alias in the van, that Jerome Knollings?"

"Nada. He's disappeared."

"Or maybe he's simply gone back to using his real name?" Brayden gave that some thought. "Find a current address on Trevor Chapman and run a check on him. Find out if he was out of town recently, specifically if he made any trips anywhere on the East Coast."

"Trevor Chapman," Garrett repeated. "As in Dana's former client."

Not a question, an objection.

"Yes. The brother of the man Ashley and she were supposed to meet the night she was killed," Brayden unnecessarily confirmed.

He appreciated his brother's concern, he really did, but he didn't need Garrett to run interference for him on this one. "I know you're trying to help," Brayden assured him. "But this isn't the way. If I look

hard enough, this time I might find that all of this comes together."

Thankfully, his brother didn't remind him that he'd been hoping it would come together for two and a half years and it hadn't yet.

Brayden ended the call and went back into the room. But after realizing he had yet another task on his hands, he paused in the doorway, took a deep breath and let it out slowly. Somehow, he needed to convince Ashley to go to bed and get some sleep.

"I thought you said you believed the property manager's explanation of what happened?" Ashley commented. "Yet, you just told your brother to check out Trevor Chapman."

Brayden lifted an eyebrow.

"I overheard you talking to Garrett," she said quickly. "And don't give me that evil eyebrow. You would have done the same thing in my position."

Since it was true, Brayden just lowered his evil eyebrow and stared at her.

"So, why do you want to check on Trevor?" Ashley asked. "You think he has something to do with this?"

"You know Trevor better than I do. What do you think?" Brayden sat down in the chair across from her. "You think he could arrange for some coincidences, like a candle and flowers in your bathtub? The fire started by the candle at your house in Virginia?"

"My first reaction is to say no, that if anyone's responsible, then it's his brother. Hyatt's the one with

the short fuse. Trevor just follows orders. Hyatt's orders. Of course, I haven't seen either of them since the trial, and people change. I suppose Trevor could now be as potentially lethal as Hyatt."

Yes. Lethal was the right word.

There was no doubt in Brayden's mind that Hyatt had been the instigator in the assault that'd nearly left Miles Granville dead. And if Hyatt had done that brutal assault, it wasn't a stretch to believe he'd go after a woman that he believed had wronged him. In Hyatt's eyes, Ashley had seriously screwed up by not getting him an acquittal.

And those suppositions always brought Brayden back to the *big* question. A question he'd asked himself at least a million times. Had Hyatt been angry enough with Ashley to pick up a high-powered rifle, aim it at an unarmed defenseless woman and fire three shots?

Had Hyatt killed Dana?

That's where the dot connections got a little fuzzy.

Since Hyatt had just escaped from jail, maybe he'd talked his wimp of a brother, Trevor, into doing the shooting for him? That way, Hyatt could stay in hiding.

Or maybe it was neither of the bothers.

Maybe it was Miles Granville, the other victim in this tangled web. Brayden had never ruled out the man because Granville had been just as angry with Ashley as Hyatt had been. Maybe even more so.

After all, she'd defended the man who had tried to kill him.

That gave Miles Granville one powerful motive. Plus, like Trevor, Granville had no alibi for the night of Dana's murder. Still, motive and lack of alibi didn't close a case. Simply put, there was no evidence against any of the three men.

And like Ashley, Miles had been in hiding since Dana's death. A name change. A new residence. Serious security precautions. And even though Brayden knew the man still lived in San Antonio, Miles kept a low profile. That didn't exclude him as the stalker, but he seemed more of a victim than a perpetrator.

Ashley's laptop was on the coffee table between them, and she used her foot to move it closer to him. "The files you asked Garrett to get are all in there. And do us both a favor and don't ask how I got them."

Oh, hell.

He hadn't wanted to get into this with her. Not tonight. Not ever. And he *really* didn't want to know what she was doing with those files.

"I've been trying to connect the dots, too," Ashley added. She paused, obviously waiting for him to respond. When he didn't—well, except for a scowl—she continued. "Aren't you even going to ask if I've had any luck?"

His scowl only got worse. "No."

"Well, I haven't. I think Hyatt's behind this, but maybe I feel that way because it's what I want to be-

lieve. Somehow, it's easier to have a face, a name, for Dana's killer, even if no one can find him."

Well, it wasn't easier for him. Name or no name, he hadn't been able to bring his wife's killer to justice. That fact was always there. Always.

The ultimate failure for a cop.

"Well?" she prompted, tipping her head to the laptop. "Are you going to open those files?"

Brayden toyed with the idea of doing just that, but he knew if he did, it would only delay her going to bed. She looked exhausted, and it was too late to rehash what wouldn't be a quick hashing of those old files.

"When you interrogated me that night," she continued, obviously ignoring his every verbal and nonverbal cue. "Or rather when you took my statement, you asked why I'd gone to that meeting with Hyatt."

"You had it right the first time. It was an interrogation. One I shouldn't have been doing."

And that's why the captain and Garrett had literally dragged him out of that interview room. However, the damage had been done. He'd put Ashley through a good fifteen minutes of hell, treating her like a criminal instead of a woman who'd just lost her sister.

Since reliving all of that turned his stomach, Brayden tried another of those verbal cues. "Why don't you go to bed? Get some rest."

He got up, thinking she'd follow his lead, but Ashley just sat there staring at him. "I went to the meet-

ing with Hyatt because he said he needed legal counsel. And I also went because I wanted to talk him into giving himself up. I knew it'd look better for him, and for me, if he turned himself in before the cops found him."

"Ashley—"

"But I also went out of a warped sense of duty. I was his lawyer, his old friend, and he asked me to meet him. And he asked Dana, of course. He said he had some concerns that involved both of us. That's where the warped part really comes into play. I didn't tell her about Hyatt's shaky psych eval because it was confidential. Because he was my client, not hers. Because he begged me not to tell anyone. But I should have told Dana. Looking back, I wish I'd done everything in my power to keep her from going with me that night."

Brayden cursed. "Ashley, I can't give you what you want. I'm sorry. But I just can't forgive you."

"I know. The truth is—I want you to blame me. It's easier that way. Easier if you hate me."

He shook his head and cursed again. "I don't hate you."

"It's easier if you don't forgive me because then I don't have to forgive myself." Tears shimmered in her eyes. Tears she tried to wipe away with that bruised hand.

Oh, hell.

He wanted to reach out to her. And maybe pull her into his arms. To comfort her. It made him ache to

see her this way. But more than his need to comfort her, and more than his need to lessen the hurt, he needed space. Because he couldn't take any more of this. So, instead of touching her, Brayden crammed his hands into his pockets.

What he couldn't do was make himself turn away.

Or stop himself from listening.

"Each night, I replay the moments leading up to the shooting," she went on, her voice fragile now. "Except I change things. I make things right. I'm the one who drives there—alone. I'm the one who steps out of that car. I'm the one who ends up on that sidewalk. And I'm the one who dies."

Brayden had his own version of that night. One where he arrived in time to save Dana. To save the day. To arrest Hyatt—or whomever was responsible. And then he took his wife home and they lived happily ever after.

"You've put yourself in purgatory," Brayden mumbled.

"Well, yeah. But I have company, right? *You.*" Now she got up, adjusted her sweater and hitched her thumb toward the laptop. "The file is in the 'pending cases' folder."

She'd already turned to leave when the phone on the end table rang. Since it was too late for social calls or telemarketers, Brayden figured it was family, job or emergency. Or a combination of all three. Bracing himself for the worst, he answered it.

"Brayden, it's me—Joe."

Brayden barely heard the greeting, because in the background, he could hear his son crying. The sobs came through loud and clear over the phone line, and Brayden realized he hadn't braced nearly enough.

"What happened?" Brayden demanded.

"Nothing like what you're thinking. Calm down. Take a deep breath. Colton had a bad dream, that's all, and he's asking for you. He's pretty upset—"

That was all Joe had to say. "I'm on the way." He hadn't wanted his son to have a nightmare, but it gave him a much-needed excuse to get the heck out of there.

He *needed* to get out there.

"Wait," Joe added. "Colton said I'm to tell you something else."

Brayden listened to the request and even had Joe repeat it. No, he hadn't heard wrong.

"I'll be there in ten minutes," Brayden said, though he wasn't quite able to suppress a groan.

"Is Colton all right?" Ashley asked the moment he hung up the phone.

"He's fine. He had a bad dream."

Relief went through her eyes, and he saw her shoulders relax. "Okay, just go. I'll set the security system, and I'll be fine. Go," Ashley repeated when he didn't budge. "He wants to see you."

"Not just me," Brayden corrected, mentally re-

playing what Joe had told him. "He wants to see you, too."

"Oh."

Brayden didn't know which one of them was more surprised, but from the look on her face, Ashley won the prize.

"I'll just put on my shoes," she said, already moving in that direction.

Ashley certainly wasn't declining the request. Not that Brayden had expected her to. And while he wanted his son's request to be filled, that request didn't do much to fulfill his own needs.

So much for breathing room.

So much for space.

He'd wanted to distance himself from his problems, for at least a few hours anyway. But one of those problems, perhaps the most troubling one of them all, would be right by his side.

Chapter Nine

Ashley rushed through her shower. Rushed to dry off. Then she just kept rushing while she pulled on an ankle-length chocolate-brown skirt and an ivory cable-knit sweater.

She checked the clock again. It was nearly noon. Way too late for her not to have made more progress. And worse, after all that sleep, she still didn't feel rested. The fog was thick in her head.

The last thing she remembered after coming back from their all-night hospital visit with Colton was crashing face first on the guest bed. Where she'd apparently stayed for six straight hours. During that six hours, she'd wasted valuable time she'd needed to prepare herself for this day.

The day Colton would come home from the hospital.

It was also the day Brayden and she were supposed to do a repeat of their baby-making attempt. Best not to dwell on that, though. Lately, her body

seemed to be devoting too much attention to such matters.

Matters that involved Brayden's hands on her.

Pushing those *matters* aside, while at the same trying to put on the socks that she'd wear with her boots, Ashley hurried into the kitchen, only to find it empty.

"Brayden?" she called out.

"I'm in the bedroom."

At the sound of his voice, she practically sprinted down the hall toward his room. "Why didn't you wake me?" Ashley asked, finger-combing her wet hair. She leaned her back against the doorjamb so she could put on her other sock.

He was at the desk, gulping down some coffee, the phone tucked against his shoulder. His attention wasn't on the coffee, the phone call or even her. It was on his computer screen. Not Dana's file, she noticed, but an e-mail of what appeared to be police work. Work with the bold word PRIORITY at the top of the page.

Ashley didn't even want to speculate about how far behind he was because of Colton's situation. Brayden was an important man in SAPD, head of Homicide, and homicides didn't stop simply because his attention was required elsewhere.

"You needed some rest," he explained in answer to her question.

He needed his rest, as well, but he'd probably gotten far less sleep than she had. He looked exhausted. And worse. He looked weary.

His hair was still damp, probably from a recent shower, but he'd skipped the shave. Desperado stubble shadowed his chin. It matched the smudgy lack-of-sleep shadows beneath his eyes. Somehow, even with all that and the rumpled jeans and cotton shirt, he managed to look, well, hot.

Of course, she was beginning to think it was a normal occurrence for Brayden to look hot.

Mercy.

Lusting after her former brother-in-law.

It could only lead to more feelings of guilt and that was something she didn't need. She had enough guilt to last her a couple of lifetimes.

"You should have gotten me up sooner." Hoping the clock in the guest room was wrong, she checked the time on the bottom panel of his computer. Nope. It wasn't wrong. "Aren't we supposed to pick up Colton in a half hour?"

"I talked to his doctor a little while ago. Colton's release has been delayed."

Well, her lust guilt were replaced with a rush of undiluted panic. Hopefully, Colton hadn't gotten sick after they'd left.

Brayden lifted his index finger in a wait-a-minute gesture and readjusted the phone so the speaker portion was closer to his mouth.

"Yes, that's right," he said to the person on the line. "The physician filling in for Dr. Underwood gave me your number."

Dr. Underwood. So, the call was about the insemination and not Colton. Ashley didn't know whether to be relieved or not. Apparently nothing serious had happened to Colton, or Brayden would have been at the hospital.

While he listened to the caller, Brayden typed in something on the computer—an e-mail response regarding a homicide—and hit the send button. He scrolled down to the next e-mail in the inbox.

"I'm trying to confirm the time and the place," Brayden continued. Again, not to her. To the person on the phone. "When I spoke to the doctor a couple of hours ago, he was still setting everything up."

Yep. She'd been right. Brayden had gotten less sleep than she had. In fact, he'd probably gotten *no* sleep. Instead, he'd been fighting through red tape, and she should have been fighting right alongside him.

"Okay," he said several moments later. Not a plain okay either, but a surprised one. "Yes, that's fine. Thanks for your help."

He clicked off the phone, gave her a glance and tackled the e-mail again. "Colton's doctor wants to give him another checkup. Nothing major, but he can't be at the hospital until at least four. We can pick up Colton right after the doctor's finished."

Ashley nodded, relieved that it wasn't a serious delay. "What was that about confirming a time and a place?"

"For the repeat insemination. I finally found a

doctor. She's on staff at a hospital across town, but she's willing to come here to the house to do it."

"Oh. Okay." She hoped she didn't sound disappointed. "How long did it take for you to arrange that?"

"Most of the morning. Not too many physicians are available on a weekend for what's considered a routine procedure. Plus, there was a liability problem with using hospital facilities. The doctor finally decided the only way we could get this done today was for her to make a house call. I'm just thankful she was willing to do it. Oh, and I did a background check on her, and she has great references. A top-notch OB-GYN, so we're not getting a quack."

Great. He'd spent all morning on the phone rather than sleep. And all so he wouldn't have to do a repeat performance with her.

She understood that.

But it still hurt.

Worse, Ashley didn't want to think about why it hurt. Fortunately, Brayden quickly gave her something else to consider.

He extracted a photo from the stack of papers on his desk and passed it to her. "Recognize him?"

Ashley studied his face before glancing at the grainy photo. This definitely wasn't about the insemination. This was about the stalker.

She took a deep breath and let it out slowly.

It was a photo taken at an ATM machine. The guy was a white male. But that was about all she could

determine. He wore a baseball cap, and he had the brim pulled down to cover his forehead. It also created a dark blotch over the lower part of his face.

"Who is he?" she asked.

"Jerome Knollings. Or whatever his real name is. He's our van driver who cruised past the house night before last."

Her gaze fired to the photo again for a more careful examination. It didn't help. If it was Hyatt, Trevor or Miles, they'd disguised their appearance.

Which wasn't a comforting thought.

Ashley shook her head, wishing that she could put a name on that face. "What about the woman up the street that you mentioned, the one who'd recently taken out a restraining order—maybe this is the guy she's trying to restrain?"

"We're looking into that."

"But it's probably not him?"

He didn't answer. Brayden simply made a sound that could have meant anything. Or nothing.

When he started to dial another number, Ashley caught his hand.

"Let me give you a situation report, lieutenant. You've had no sleep. You're under extreme stress. And your little boy is coming home in a couple of hours. Put Jerome Knollings on the back burner and take a nap."

But he didn't. Brayden just sat there and rubbed his other hand over his face. "I can't—"

"You can. Colton's going to need you, and you'll be absolutely no good to him if you don't rest."

"I need to make another call."

"I'll do that for you," she insisted.

He shook his head. "It's about the, uh, collection part of the insemination."

Ashley had already opened her mouth to interrupt him again, but she stopped. Well, that *uh* stopped her anyway. "What about it? Is there a problem?"

"The doctor suggested I do the collection here. To save some time. I need to find out how far in advance, or if she just wants me to wait until she arrives."

"And just when is she supposed to arrive?"

"That's the up-in-the-air part, but she thought she could be here in about two hours. If not, then it'll have to be tonight after she's made rounds at the hospital."

Ashley went through a mental timetable. With the collection, waiting for the doctor to arrive and the procedure itself, it could pose logistics problems for picking up Colton. Or worse, Colton's welcome home might even be cut short because of the procedure. Cut short so Brayden could avoid touching her.

In addition to making her feel like a leper, all these arrangements were starting to rile her. "So, let me get this straight. Even though you're exhausted and even though the insemination might interfere with your plans to pick up your son, you're going to go through with it anyway?"

Ashley didn't finish the rest of that thought. Didn't

want to finish it. Because it was a ridiculous objection. Of course, Brayden didn't want to touch her.

She shouldn't have wanted to touch him, either.

But she apparently did.

And that riled her even more.

Mercy, she was stupid. Her body was stupid. Her thoughts were stupid. Why was she having these feelings anyway? They made no sense. None. And one way or another, she intended to rid herself of them.

Brayden hissed out his breath. "Ashley, I didn't—"

"Forget what I just said. Blame it on fatigue. Coffee deprivation. Full moon. Take your pick, and just forget about it." Ashley paused only a second. "Listen, do the collection, give it to me, along with the phone number of the doctor, and I'll take care of the rest. You'll pick up Colton."

"You're upset."

Not with him. But herself. "You didn't listen to what I said. You were supposed to take your pick. My advice? Blame it on the lack of coffee because I'm in dire need. Which is my reminder to grab a cup while you're taking care of that collection."

She turned to leave, but he latched onto her arm. "Why are you so upset?"

Except he didn't ask. He demanded. There was anger in it. And the fatigue that'd been on his face just moments earlier had dissolved. In its place, Ashley saw the effects of that anger. His iron jaw. Tight mouth. Narrowed eyes. Even his nostrils flared.

"Why are *you* so upset?" Ashley countered, certain she was exhibiting some of those same facial anger indicators as well.

"Because I know what you're thinking."

"I seriously doubt that." She jerked her arm from his grip, turned and actually made it a step before he caught her. Brayden whirled her back around to face him.

Not gently, either.

He leaned closer. Too close. Right in her personal space. "I'm not—"

"Interested," she interrupted. "I know. Neither am I. So, whatever you feel you have to say, keep it to yourself."

Amazingly, his jaw got even tighter. "No."

"No?" she questioned, surprised.

"No. Because there's no reason for you to be hurt—"

She slung off his grip again so she could throw her hands in the air. "Now, we're talking about hurt? I don't think so." Ashley huffed. "Can we just *please* drop this?"

He didn't.

He caught her arm again. Ashley tried to get out of his grip—again. Brayden didn't budge.

Neither did she.

She spun around, moving him with her, and his back landed hard against the wall. It didn't put any distance between them since he took hold of her other arm, holding her in place.

Right in front of him.

Looking at him wasn't something she needed at this particular moment. Their anger took on an edge, a dangerous edge. One that stirred things deep inside her. It broke down boundaries that were better left well-defined.

My, the thoughts she had. Bad thoughts. That involved her putting her mouth to his and taking everything.

"Brayden," she warned.

The grip he had on her melted. He lowered his hands, pressed the back of his head against the wall and groaned. He opened his mouth to say something but then apparently changed his mind.

Okay. The boundaries were still intact, for the most part. With the exception of those troubling thoughts. And that was her signal to leave. Ashley turned, but Brayden slid his arms around her waist and pulled her closer until her back was against his chest.

Not the best of positions.

Not with them touching.

He was solid. Not in a bulky buffed-up sort of way. Lean. Strong.

Warm.

Definitely warm.

His breath hit against her neck. It was hot. Quick. His pulse and heartbeat must have been pounding because she could feel it everywhere they touched.

Or maybe that was her own heartbeat.

It was impossible to tell, since they were so close. Plastered against each other, it was also hard to tell where his body ended and hers began.

It was hard to tell a lot of things.

Except his scent.

That scent was distinctive. Unforgettable. Something dark and male. Definitely not tame. Dangerous, even. Yet, it stirred her blood. Stirred her body.

And the heat rolled through her.

Ashley closed her eyes, slowly, afraid that Brayden would maneuver her around so she'd have to face him. She wasn't sure she could do that. But he didn't maneuver her anywhere. He kept the pseudoembrace, even tightened it, and he put his mouth against her hair.

Not a kiss. Just a touch of his mouth. A touch that kicked up that heat a notch.

It was wrong to want him. So wrong. But it didn't matter. Because Ashley didn't stop. Neither did Brayden. He moved his body forward, pressing hard against her. And not just hard. Aroused.

She could feel him. Every inch of him. That hard ridge straining in front of his jeans. How would it feel if he took her right there?

Ashley wanted to be disgusted with herself. With him. But that wasn't the reaction she had. Far from it. She wanted more. She wanted him.

She wanted Brayden.

Ashley leaned back, angling herself, sliding her

right hip against his erection. Slowly. Deliberately. Knowing exactly what she was doing to him.

What she was doing to herself.

She angled her head, too, so that his mouth wasn't on her hair, but on the side of her face. Warm flesh against warm flesh. Still not a kiss, but it was just as effective. Maybe more. Because this was forbidden. Taboo. And for some reason that only made her want him more.

Brayden released the hold he had on her waist. His hand skimmed down her left hip, and he caught a handful of her skirt. Gathering it up. Tugging. Pulling. Dragging the fabric and his fingers along the outside of her bare thigh.

It lit a dozen fires along the way.

He didn't stop there.

With his mouth still on her cheek, moving and pressing, he slid his hand across her thigh to the front of her panties, hooked his fingers onto the elastic.

And he slipped his hand inside.

Ashley arched her back and moaned.

This wasn't some test, like the night before, to make sure she was ready for him.

Not this.

This had an entirely different purpose. He eased his hand between her legs so he could slide his fingers over that sensitive bud of flesh and slip them inside her. This was meant to pleasure her, and it worked.

It. Worked.

The world blurred. Her body turned soft. Preparing itself. For him. For Brayden.

Because she suddenly wanted him more than her next breath, Ashley didn't voice the objection waiting in the back of her mind. Instead, she let him touch her.

Rough, almost frantic slippery strokes.

While his mouth feasted on her cheek and neck. While his erection pressed against her thigh. Until she couldn't think. Until she couldn't breathe.

He didn't stop there.

Brayden kept touching. Kept pleasuring her. His thumb brushing high against the most aroused part of her, while those clever fingers found a different spot. Inside her. Inches inside her. Stroking it, too. In perfect rhythm with the movements of his thumb.

Ashley felt her legs give way. And she was falling. Except she didn't. Brayden didn't let her fall. He was right there to catch her.

They both sank to the carpeted floor on their knees, with him still behind her. With her leaning against the bed. With him leaning against her. With him still touching her with those maddening strokes.

The fire blazed through her, and she reached for him. Sliding her hand over the front of his jeans. Matching his strokes with some of her own. Until the pace was frantic. Unbearable. Until it took them to a place where mere strokes were no longer enough.

Not nearly enough.

She wanted him inside her. Fully inside her. Every rock-hard inch of him. Just like this. With them on the floor. With him behind her. She wanted the feel of those toned abs pressing against her buttocks. She wanted friction. Heat. The slide of his erection against the very places he was touching.

Ashley reached for his zipper, but he stopped her. He put his hand over hers and stopped her. Ashley might have protested. *Might.* If he hadn't quickened those strokes with his fingers inside her. If she hadn't felt his tongue on her neck. He sucked gently but in just the right spot.

"Let me feel you against my hand," he whispered.

She heard the words. Felt him say them since his mouth was still on her neck. And she responded. She couldn't help but respond. All doubts faded.

All coherent thoughts disappeared.

With each new stroke, each frantic thrust of his fingers, her body slipped into a spiral. The pressure built. The need commanded. Consumed. Until all she could hear was Brayden.

Let me feel you.

Let me feel you.

Ashley stopped fighting to hold on. She no longer wanted to hold on. She let him take her to the only place she wanted to go.

Need surged one last time. There was one last stroke. One last whisper.

And Ashley let herself fall.

Brayden was right there to catch her.

IT TOOK ASHLEY several long moments to climb out of that spiral and come back to earth. Even then, the world seemed as if it had turned on its axis.

Her breathing was labored. Her pulse, jumping. But little by little, her body began to return to normal.

Well, as normal as it would ever be, considering.

"I owed you that," Brayden said, his voice hardly more than a whisper. "After the way I took you last night, I owed you that."

Those words had to make it through the thick layers of sensations still racking her body. But they did. Eventually they got through.

With amazing clarity.

Along with that clarity, she felt a slam of anger.

Ashley rolled out of his embrace. Away from him. And stared at him. "A pity orgasm? Great, just great."

"I didn't mean that, and you know it."

Did she?

"This was such a mistake," she countered. "Top of the list of dumb things to do."

Brayden backed away from her, as well. "You're right. Not very smart. If you want to blame someone, blame me."

"Oh, I do." She didn't, of course. But it didn't matter. Right now the only thing that mattered was get-

ting away from him. Then, she could try to figure out why she'd just done something so incredibly stupid.

She didn't have time to contemplate that, or anything else. Brayden didn't even have time for a comeback, though he certainly looked as if he was gearing up for one.

The doorbell rang.

Lousy timing. If it had rung just ten minutes earlier Brayden wouldn't have managed to get his hands in her pants, and she wouldn't be feeling like an idiot.

"That's probably the doctor," he grumbled.

When he got to his feet, Ashley couldn't help but notice that he was aroused. Seriously aroused. Worse, he noticed that she noticed.

"Well, you shouldn't have any trouble doing the collection," she said under her breath. "So, I guess we accomplished something. Glad I could help."

His eyes darkened, and he had to unclench his teeth before he could speak. "Pity foreplay?"

Ashley was sure her eyes did some darkening, as well. "You can call it what you want. I'm not the one who scheduled the insemination."

"I didn't schedule it because I don't want you," Brayden informed her, and then headed for the door. "I scheduled it because I do."

Chapter Ten

Brayden bracketed his hands against the shower wall and let the water pound down on his neck and back. It helped with the knotted muscles. It even helped a little with the bone-weary fatigue.

It didn't help anything else.

He'd violated rules. Personal rules. There was already enough conflict between Ashley and him without adding sex to the mix. Yet, he'd added it. And it didn't matter that it was one-sided. It was still intimate contact that he should have done everything in his power to avoid.

Instead, he'd instigated it.

Brayden cursed and turned his face toward the hard spray of water. He could have dismissed the time in her laundry room as a necessity. And he had dismissed it. But what he'd done in his bedroom with Ashley wasn't a dismissing kind of thing, and it certainly wasn't a necessity. Even though it had felt like it at the time.

A pity orgasm, she'd called it.

Hell, he only wished that were true.

He could handle feeling pity for her far better than he could handle feeling anything else. Because that *anything else* was beginning to encompass emotions he should never feel. That damn sure wasn't why he'd brought her here. This was about saving Colton, and if he had to tattoo that onto his forehead, or another specific part of him, he would remember it.

Deciding the doctor should be done with the insemination by now, Brayden turned off the shower and got dressed. He took his time, though, mainly because he figured both Ashley and he would need it before facing each other. Thanks to him and that so-called pity orgasm, he'd made things practically unbearable between them.

Brayden stepped out of the bathroom, paused and listened. No sound of voices. No sound of anything. When he went to the living room and glanced out the window, he saw that the doctor's car was no longer parked in front of the house.

"She left right after the procedure," he heard Ashley say from behind him.

She was in the hall, just outside the guest room door. She, too, was dressed. She even had on her coat. And her suitcase was in her hand.

"Everything went like clockwork," Ashley explained. She stepped closer. But not too close. And

she maneuvered the suitcase so that it was between them. "The doctor wished us good luck."

Brayden nodded, suddenly not caring what the doctor said, and he tipped his head to the suitcase. "What's this about?"

"I'm going home." She pressed her lips together for a moment. "It's time, Brayden."

Man, he'd seriously blown it.

He'd expected Ashley to keep her distance, but he hadn't expected to send her on the run. He had some fast-talking to do if he hoped to convince her to stay put. And then he'd have to do more fast-talking to explain to himself why he wanted her to stay.

She walked to the window. Not the one next to him, but the one on the other side of the room. As far away from him as she could get while remaining in the same general vicinity. She looked out. "I made reservations for a flight that leaves in a little over two hours. But I'd like to swing by and see Colton on the way to the airport."

Yes. It would give her time for that but little else, since it meant she'd need to leave immediately.

"Ashley—"

"I called your sister," she interrupted, obviously ignoring him. "Katelyn volunteered to drive me. Oh, and I arranged to have a Christmas tree delivered. I figured Colton would like that."

Brayden stepped in front of her when she tried to

walk past him to get to the front door. "You don't have to do this."

"I do. I promised Colton that Santa would visit, and it wouldn't be a proper visit without a tree."

"That's not what I meant."

"I know. And I know you're wrong. I *do* have to do this. I have to go." There was a small sound of frustration deep in her throat. "Everything is getting jumbled here, Brayden. The candle and phone message coincidences that don't feel like coincidences. All the memories of Dana. Everything feels raw and too close to the surface. I need some space."

He nodded, unable to disagree with her about any of that. Things were jumbled. Things were raw. But he didn't think any amount of space would make that better. He'd torn down some huge boundaries in his bedroom, and there was no way to put them back in place.

Heck, he wasn't even sure he wanted them back in place.

"The doctor said I could do one of those home pregnancy kits in as early as five days." She glanced out the sidelight window by the door, obviously looking for Katelyn. "Even if it's negative, it doesn't mean we failed. It just might take an extra day or two for the test to show a positive result."

She picked up her purse from the entry table and adjusted a few strands of her hair that in no way needed an adjustment. "I'll call you when I know

something one way or the other. If there needs to be a repeat procedure, I'd like for it to be done in Virginia."

It was doable. In fact, it was more than doable since the trip to San Antonio had inconvenienced her. And worse, it might have endangered her.

But her leaving just didn't feel right.

Nothing about this felt right.

"What if the stalker follows you?" he asked.

"He won't. I'll be taking several flights to Virginia. A circuitous route. While I'm at the airport I'll make arrangements to upgrade the security system at my house. I also have some cop friends, and I'll ask them to do patrols like the ones you arranged here."

So, she'd made plans. Good plans. But not perfect ones. "And if that isn't enough?" Brayden wanted to know.

"It'll be enough. I own a gun, and I know how to use it. Besides, I've managed to keep myself safe for two and a half years."

"But the stalker didn't know where you were. Things might have changed."

Ashley huffed. "Look, Brayden, there's nothing to say. We had sex last night. Today, we played around in your bedroom, and now we both feel like hell. Deny that, and you'll be liar."

He couldn't deny it. He did feel like hell. And that feeling was increasing significantly with every word of this conversation.

"I'll drive you to the airport," he said already pulling out his phone.

"You don't have to do that. In fact, it'll be easier if you—"

"Save your breath. I'm driving you." And along the way, he might even be able to figure out how to apologize for what he'd done.

Groveling was a distinct possibility.

Thankfully, he caught Katelyn as she was on her way out the door and canceled her chauffeuring plans. He did that with Ashley glaring at him.

"That wasn't necessary," she assured him the moment he got off the phone.

"Yeah, it was. Because you see, you don't think we have to talk, but we do. And since you're determined to leave, that means we talk in the car."

She mumbled something under her breath and gave the shoulder strap of her purse an adjustment as if she'd declared war on it.

Instead of going back through the house to get to the garage, Ashley went through the front door. No blast of icy winter wind. As it was prone to do in San Antonio, the cold front had come and gone, and in its place was a cool, breezeless day. Which was good. Since he was getting more than enough iciness from her.

"I don't want to talk," Ashley said from over her shoulder.

"Tough. We're talking."

He tried to do the gentlemanly thing and take her

suitcase, but she held on tight and marched down the steps and into the front yard.

From out of the corner of his eye, Brayden saw the car approach from the left. He felt the primal warning slam through him.

But it was too late to warn Ashley.

Too late to get to her in time.

The silenced shots slashed through the air.

IT TOOK ASHLEY A SECOND to realize the sound hadn't come from the car engine. But instead, it was the sound of gunshots fired from a weapon rigged with a silencer.

With her heart leaping to her throat, she dived for the ground. On the way down, she caught a glimpse of the car, specifically its lowered window on the passenger's side. She also got a glimpse of the ski-masked shadowy figure in the driver's seat.

A man with a gun.

He fired another shot.

Not a blast. But a deadly sounding swoosh that seemed to skim right next to her head.

"Ashley," Brayden yelled. "Get down!"

She did. Ashley rolled over, tucking herself against a thick cluster of rosemary shrubs. It wasn't much protection. Not much at all.

She realized that with the next shot.

The bullet slammed into a landscape rock right in front of her and sent bits of it flying through the air.

Ashley felt the sting of the debris on her face. She felt the fear. It clawed its way through her, setting off a dozen nightmarish memories. Of another shooting. Of her sister's murder.

Brayden was suddenly right there. Scrambling along the ground toward her. He had his weapon drawn and aimed. He also had a large portion of his body exposed to the gunman.

Her fear kicked up a notch. Not because Ashley was worried about being shot, but because she was worried about Brayden. Sweet heaven. He'd put himself in the line of fire.

Ashley leaned out from her meager cover and latched onto him to pull him into the shrubs with her. He cursed at her, yelling for her to stay down. She ignored him and hauled him closer. Just as the car gunned the engine.

Before he sped away, the driver got off another shot.

This one clipped off a chunk of the rosemary, spraying them with the prickly needles.

"Were you hit?" Brayden demanded.

Fighting through the adrenaline, Ashley tried to do a quick assessment. "I don't think so. How about you?"

"Don't worry about me." He climbed over her, sheltering her body with his, while he kept his weapon pointed at the street where the gunman had launched the attack.

But not just any gunman. This almost certainly

wasn't some random act of violence. This was the stalker.

He'd found her.

And worse. He was no longer content to make harassing phone calls or leave candles burning.

Brayden unclipped his phone and pressed a button. "Lt. O'Malley. I need assistance at my residence."

She listened as he relayed the information. Other than the speed of his request, and the slight rush of his words, he gave no indication of panic.

Unlike her.

Ashley's entire body was in panic mode, and it took everything within her to make herself stay put. More than anything she wanted to latch onto Brayden and get them both inside the house.

Brayden cursed. That was the only warning she got before he pushed her head closer to the ground.

And Ashley soon realized why.

There was a high-pitched squeal of tires. The smell of rubber burning against asphalt. Another slam of adrenaline surged through her.

Another shot.

Even though she couldn't see the car, Ashley knew it was the same gunman. It was the same gun. The same silenced rounds of fire. And any one of those deadly rounds could kill Brayden or her.

Brayden levered himself slightly above her and aimed. He got off a shot. It crashed through the back glass of the car just as it sped away again.

"Backup's on the way," Brayden let her know.

Under the circumstances, waiting for backup was all they could do. They couldn't try to go inside the house or even to the garage. They were literally half-way between them, and that meant they were only halfway to safety. Which was no safety at all since the gunman could be out there, waiting for them to make a move.

So they stayed put. There on the ground. With her heart in her throat.

Long, agonizing moments passed before she heard the police sirens. Longer moments still before Ashley realized the gunman was done for the day.

But just for today.

He'd be back.

And what small sanctuary she'd managed to gather was gone.

Chapter Eleven

"They just drove up," Brayden's sister, Katelyn, announced.

Ashley heard the garage door grind open, and then seconds later, it closed again. She held her breath through the entire mundane process.

Praying that nothing would go wrong and that Colton and Brayden would make it safely inside. Because after the gunman's attack, nothing—including the simple opening and closing of a garage—felt mundane anymore.

Katelyn withdrew her gun from her holster and hurried to the side entrance that led to the garage.

Holding her weapon discreetly by her side, Katelyn gave Ashley an inspecting glance from over her shoulder. "Don't worry. You don't look as if you were shot at just a few hours ago."

"Good," Ashley mumbled.

But she had no idea how she'd managed that particular feat. Inside, her nerves were a tangle of fatigue and spent adrenaline.

"It's short stuff," Katelyn squealed, throwing open the door.

That was her cue. Ashley stepped back into the kitchen, as Katelyn insisted she do. Out of the potential line of sight, and fire. And she waited.

Brayden came in, carrying his son in his arms. Colton was pale but smiling. He immediately reached out and gave Katelyn a high five. In the same motion, Katelyn shut the door, locked it and ushered them into the living room. Away from the windows. A reminder that even though Ashley might not have looked it, Brayden and she had indeed been shot at earlier.

Security measures were no longer just a precaution.

They were a necessity.

"So, Colt, what do you think of your magic hideaway?" Brayden asked.

The boy's gaze skirted around the living room. "It's okay. But I'd ruther go home."

"You're joking, right?" Katelyn countered. "This place is so much better. It's got cable. Plus, I brought over a kilo of gummy bears."

Colton gave her a you-still-haven't-convinced-me shrug. Ashley understood completely. The place was nice. The house of a friend of a friend, Brayden had explained. But it wasn't home, and today should have been the day that Colton got to go home.

Thanks to the gunman, that wasn't going to happen tonight. And maybe not for a lot of nights.

Ashley stepped out from the shadows, and just as he'd done in the hospital, Colton spotted her right away.

"Aunt Ashley." Another smile. One that caused his dimples to flash. "Do you get to stay here, too?"

She nodded. "For a while."

For six days anyway. Until she knew for certain if she was pregnant. During that time, she could make plans. She could decide what to do.

Or, more specifically, she could decide what *not* to do.

One thing was for certain—it was too big a risk to return to Virginia. If the candle fire at her house was the work of the stalker, then he'd know where to find her. That meant she couldn't go back. And she couldn't stay in San Antonio, either. That would only further endanger Brayden and Colton.

That wasn't going to happen if she could stop it.

And she could stop it by leaving.

If she made arrangements for a new place, a new start, and just vanished, then maybe the stalker would crawl back under the same rock he'd been hiding under for the past two and a half years.

Brayden carried his son to the sofa and placed him amid the bedding and pillows that Ashley had arranged. When he took his sister aside to whisper something to her, Ashley walked closer to Colton.

"Will you be here for Christmas?" he asked.

"Maybe," she lied.

Christmas was definitely out since it was still twelve

days away. Practically an eternity. By then, she'd have the pregnancy-test results and would have already picked out a spot where she could escape so she could either have the baby or wait for reinsemination.

Ashley sat down on the coffee table across from him. "But even if I'm not here, I'll make sure Santa visits. And don't worry because there's not a chimney. Your dad will let Santa in so he can leave the presents. Lots and lots of presents."

Colton's eyes brightened. "How many is lots and lots?"

"More than you can count." She paused, eyeing his dimpled grin. "Just how high can you count anyway?"

"To twenty, but maybe I can learn some bigger numbers before Christmas."

Ashley laughed and made a mental note to do some quick shopping on the Internet.

She glanced back at Brayden when he touched her arm. "Could we talk?"

"Sure." She brushed a kiss on Colton's forehead and followed Brayden down the hall.

"Are you okay?" he asked once they were inside one of the bedrooms.

Ashley leaned against the dresser and let it support her. "Not really, but under the circumstances, I'm doing about as well as I can manage."

Brayden walked closer, just a few quiet steps, and examined her eyes. "Have you *managed* yourself enough for a good ass chewing?"

Okay. So, she hadn't expected hugs and reassurances, but she hadn't expected that, either. "Do I have a reason to have such a chewing?"

"Absolutely. What you did in that yard was stupid." That earned her a gentle but authoritative poke in the chest with his index finger. "You should have never left cover to get me. *Never.* You could have been killed."

"Ditto."

He blinked. "Ditto?"

"D-i-t-t-o," Ashley spelled out. "Did you just expect me to stay hidden in the rosemary bushes and not try to help you? Especially since the only reason you were in danger in the first place was because you were helping me?"

"I'm a cop," Brayden said as if that explained everything, which it didn't.

"Well, yeah, but that doesn't mean bullets will bounce right off of your thick, impervious hide. And please don't turn this into a male-female, protector of the universe kind of argument because that would just seriously piss me off."

"No argument." She could see the pulse hammer in his neck. And his veins, practically bulging. "What you did was stupid, and I thought we'd already agreed you wouldn't do anything stupid."

She groaned. "Okay. This is an impasse, which normally wouldn't bother me, but if we don't get past this, I won't be able to get you into bed." She

quickly lifted her finger to indicate a P.S. was on its way. "And by that, I mean get you to go to bed— *alone*. For sleeping purposes."

"The impasse stays an impasse until you realize you can't put yourself in danger."

"Then, an impasse it is. Because it was stupid for you to put yourself between those bullets and me. Brave, yes. But stupid, too."

"It wasn't brave," Brayden countered, rubbing his hand over his face. "Bravery is for people who have a choice about what to do. I didn't. I'm a cop. I re-acted exactly how I've been trained to react. No choice involved."

Ashley gave him what she hoped was a blank look. "Is that BS meter in your head going nuts? Because mine sure is. I know for a fact SAPD doesn't train cops to jump out in front of bullets. Don't," Ashley cautioned when he opened his mouth, probably to continue his argument. "Just accept my thanks, toss in a lukewarm you're-welcome, and leave our impasse at that."

He nodded. Eventually. "You're welcome."

But he didn't leave it at that.

He reached out, slowly, as if he might change his mind at any moment. However, he didn't change his mind. He didn't stop. Brayden pulled her to him and took her in his arms. Not for carnal purposes. No ro-mance involved. That strong, warm embrace was meant to comfort her, to reassure her, to promise that he would do everything possible to keep her safe.

It felt like heaven.

Worse, it felt right.

Against her better judgment, Ashley went with it. She stood there and took everything he was offering. Even though what he was offering had a huge price tag on it. Instead of the distance she'd hoped to keep between them, that embrace brought her closer to him. Not just physically, but in ways they should be avoiding.

"You should get some rest," she murmured, forcing herself to move away.

Brayden held on. Not a forceful hold, either. He simply didn't let go of her. "I need you to cooperate, to stay here," he said, his voice a hoarse whisper. "Until I can make things safe."

Ashley didn't even consider telling him she planned to do the same thing—to make things safe. Not with that plea and exhaustion in his tone. Nor would she mention their concepts of what constituted safe might not be the same.

For now, she simply nodded.

He drew in a slow breath and released it just as slowly. Then he let go of her.

"One of the neighbors saw the car speeding away." Another deep breath, and Brayden sat on the edge of the bed. "It scraped against a fire hydrant when it clipped the curve. So now, we have paint shavings. We might get lucky and get a match."

What he wasn't saying was the car was probably

a rental. Or stolen. The stalker almost certainly hadn't used his own vehicle for a drive-by shooting. Still, that wasn't necessarily a dead end. If they could trace those paint shavings, they might be able to get prints from the car. If they could find the car, that is.

So many if's.

"I put Miles Granville and Trevor Chapman under surveillance," he continued. "I should have done it sooner. If I had, that shooting might not have happened today."

Mercy. She hated to see him beat himself up like this. "Hindsight, huh? I've heard it's twenty-twenty. Too bad the rest of us mere mortals have to deal with plain old ordinary sight." Ashley reached over, turned out the lights and pointed to the bed. "Now, get some sleep."

"Not—"

"I need you to cooperate, to stay here," she said, repeating his earlier request verbatim. "Katelyn and I will take care of Colton. Everything will be all right."

The last part was more hope than assurance, and both of them knew it.

Nothing would be all right ever again.

Nothing.

Until the stalker was stopped.

A NIGHTMARE WOKE BRAYDEN. Or rather *the* nightmare. The one where he'd arrived on the scene just

seconds after the bullets were fired. Seconds after Dana was hit. Seconds after she'd died.

Except this nightmare was different.

It wasn't just Dana on that sidewalk in a pool of blood, but Ashley, as well. He'd been seconds too late to save either of them, and because of that, they were both dead.

With his heart still pounding in his throat and his body braced for a long-lost fight, Brayden threw back the covers and got up. He checked the time—just past midnight. And he listened for a moment. Assessing. Trying to decide if all was as it should be. It was.

Everything was quiet.

Except for the steady drum of his pulse in his head.

He pulled on his jeans and went down the hall to check on Colton. And Ashley. He found them both in Colton's temporary bedroom. Both asleep. Thanks to the cheery frog night-light, he could see his son snuggled under the covers, and Ashley was in the chair next to the bed. She'd slumped over, her head on the edge of Colton's pillow.

Colton was holding her hand.

Brayden hadn't expected such a simple thing to latch onto his heart. But, man, it did. Mainly because he knew it wasn't such a simple thing. Ashley was reaching out to his son, in more ways than one. In more ways than he'd ever imagined she would.

And maybe not just reaching out to Colton.

But to him, as well.

Soon, he'd have to sort out how he felt about that. But first he had to do whatever it took to keep them safe.

Not wanting to disturb them, Brayden stepped out of the room, but the movement must have alerted Ashley because she lifted her head from the pillow. Her gaze searched the room and landed on him.

She smiled. It was drowsy and ripe with sleep. She pushed herself out of the chair and practically stumbled toward him.

"Did you get some rest?" she murmured, sliding her hair away from her face. Her fingers slipped through the strands and came to rest on the back of her neck.

He nodded. "You?"

"Some. Colton was a little nervous about the strange room so he asked me to stay in here with him."

Something he should have been doing for his son. It should have felt wrong for Ashley to take his place. But it didn't.

God forbid, it didn't.

Her red silk pj's whispered against his arm when she stepped into the hall with him and partially shut the door. She smelled good. Not a man-made scent from a bottle or from a bar of soap. But her own unique scent. A smell that would always remind him of having sex with her.

Of course, a lot of things reminded him of that.

He'd never kissed her. An odd thought considering the sudden ache he had for her was below the belt

and not above it. Except the ache seemed to be spreading. To his mouth. To his hands.

To his heart.

Brayden quickly pushed that last thought aside.

Dana's death had broken his heart, and he wasn't ready to risk that kind of pain again. Hell, he wasn't sure he'd ever be ready.

Except his body disagreed with that, too.

He suddenly felt ready—for a lot of things. Of course, that probably had something to do with the fact that Ashley was standing only inches from him, looking far better than he wanted her to look.

"Did you want something?" she asked.

An honest question, with no carnal undertones whatsoever, but Brayden couldn't help it. He made a tortured sound of amusement. Dark, ironic amusement.

"Oh," she said, flexing her eyebrows. She covered what would have almost certainly been a laugh with a soft cough.

"Oh," he confirmed.

"Would it help if I told you what you *want* is probably a deeply rooted primal instinct that you have no control over? Because you know I'm ovulating, your male body is gearing up to make certain you impregnate me and thereby insure the continuation of the human species."

"Well, that certainly takes the emotion out of it," Brayden lied.

"I didn't figure we were ready to deal with the emotion."

"True."

Neither of them was ready. Might never be. But that didn't stop him from wanting his hands on her. Her hands on him. It would have taken a much stronger man to turn away.

Brayden reached out and did what he'd almost certainly regret.

He pulled her to him.

And the battle started.

The air between them changed immediately. Sizzled. As if the atoms and molecules had switched to double time.

He thought of plenty of reasons why he shouldn't look down at her, why he should back away. The need for him to remain objective and focused. The need to keep his distance. Their past. Their uncertain future.

They were all good solid reasons.

And yet none of them stopped him.

She looked up at him. But not with any ordinary look. *The* look. Her eyes were crying out with need for comfort. And more. Much more.

Her breath was already thin and fast, and it was getting faster. He saw the pulse hammer in her delicate throat. He felt her heart pound against his. And the air just kept on sizzling.

Brayden stared down at her. Somewhere amid that

long, smoldering look, he got lost in the depths of her blue eyes. And her scent. Man, that scent. All woman. It spoke to him in ways nothing else could have.

Her touch didn't help things, either. She slid her fingers along his biceps. A sensual, slow caress. That wasn't all. Moving even closer, she brushed her hip against the front of his jeans. Yep. There it was. The metaphorical striking match. It fired his blood. But even then, he could have stopped.

Probably.

But he didn't. He waited, bracing himself.

He didn't brace himself nearly enough.

His mouth came to hers. Her lips pressed against his, taking. Not a soft gentle kiss of comfort. Not this. There was no comfort in the sensual moves of her mouth. This was all white-hot heat, fueled with lethal adrenaline and raw emotion.

The waiting was over. The battle, lost. But a new one began.

The sensations slammed through him. Fast. Hard. Strong. Resisting wasn't possible. So he took everything she offered. Everything. And upped the stakes.

Brayden latched onto her hair with one hand, the back of her neck with the other, and hauled her to him. Against him. Until he could feel every silky soft inch of her.

It still wasn't enough.

Not nearly enough.

Not with the ache inside him.

He savored the feel of her lips against his. Soft. Like warm silk. She responded and moved with him. He tested the taste of her, touching his tongue to hers. Like her scent, it went straight through him. Like fire. Like something he desperately needed.

Because he felt as if he might drown in that need, Brayden put a choke hold on his body and eased back slightly.

"Was that part of those primal instincts?" Ashley whispered against his mouth.

"It was a mistake."

She shook her head. The movement brushed her lips against his. Her hair slid over his cheek. "It didn't feel like a mistake."

"I know. That's why it was one."

Because he was standing so close to her, he felt her stiffen slightly. Ashley backed up a step. But Brayden quickly recaptured that ground.

He slipped his hand around the back of her neck and hauled her to him. He recaptured her mouth, as well. Not to taste, experience or touch. But to take. To feast.

Ashley did her own share of feasting. She made a sound of pure pleasure and wound her arms around his neck. Their bodies came together. Silk and woman against his bare chest.

"Mercy." She pulled back slightly and touched her fingers to her lips. "I didn't think you'd be this good."

He groaned. "That's not the right thing to say. I don't need anything to encourage me."

"I know." She gulped in a breath and repeated it. "But let's think this through. If the other kiss was a mistake, then that one was a whopper. I'm talking huge."

"Agreed."

"And if we keep kissing, then I'll want to do something about this." Without taking her gaze from his, Ashley slid her hand over the front of his jeans and had him seeing double. "Because I have some primal instincts stirring in me, as well. And that surprises me. Because I haven't felt these specific stirrings in a long, long time."

Maybe it was because she was so honest, or maybe because she didn't move her hand even after she had proven her point. Either way, Brayden considered carrying her to his bed. Or maybe on the floor, taking her in some hard, fast, frantic coupling that would make them both come in a flash of pure heat.

He considered it.

And dismissed it.

Not easily, but he dismissed it.

Partly because his son was in the other room and might wake up. Also, because Ashley wasn't his for the taking. And his heart wasn't his for the giving.

She searched his eyes, paused, nodded. Understanding. "Good night, Brayden," she whispered.

And before he could change his mind, or do whatever it took to change hers, Ashley went into her bedroom and closed the door.

Chapter Twelve

With his brother, Garrett, standing by his side, Brayden watched the video feed as a detective questioned Trevor Chapman.

"This guy's on your shortlist of stalker suspects?" Garrett asked. The question was loaded with doubts. "He's like Forrest Gump in an expensive Italian suit."

Brayden had his own doubts, as well, and Trevor's demeanor wasn't doing a lot to dispel them. Chapman sat soldier-stiff in the chair, his hands in his lap. His double-breasted conservative suit was immaculate, pricey even, but far from fashionable. There was concern in his eyes. Sweat popping out on his forehead. He stuttered. Often. And he was respectful to the detective, calling him sir at the end of every response.

Not exactly the deportment of a gunman who'd tried to kill Ashley and him in broad daylight. That had a been a gutsy attack, and the guy sweating in the interview didn't appear to be gutsy material.

Trevor was carefully answering the detective's questions. Not vague answers, either. When the detective had asked him where he was the day before, specifically at the time of the shooting, Trevor had given a detailed account of the deal he'd been working on for his family's import business.

Maybe too detailed, Brayden wondered?

He wasn't about to discount the man just yet. Because, simply put, Trevor had no alibi for the time of Dana's shooting. But then, neither did Miles Granville, another name on Brayden's list. Granville should be arriving any minute for his own *voluntary* interview. Within an hour, Brayden might have the information necessary to stop the stalker.

Or not.

Because Trevor and Granville were on that list all right. But neither had top billing. Hyatt Chapman was firmly inked into that spot.

"Any idea where your brother, Hyatt, is?" the detective asked Trevor.

"No. I haven't seen him since he escaped." Trevor ran his hand through his prematurely thinning but perfectly styled blond hair—again—a gesture he'd repeated several times. "But he did call me about a week ago."

That captured Brayden's attention. Ashley had been back in San Antonio for a week.

"Hyatt didn't say much," Trevor continued. "And he didn't talk long. He was concerned the phone

might be tapped—even though I assured him that it wasn't. I asked him where he was staying, but he wouldn't tell me, and he'd blocked his number so it didn't show on caller ID."

"Hyatt didn't say much?" the detective repeated. "What *did* he say exactly?"

Trevor paused and tried to answer, but had to work his way through another stuttering and hair-touching bout first. "That he might be coming home soon."

The detective picked right up on that. "He does that often—calls to say he might be coming home soon?"

Trevor shook his head. "He's never done that. I don't know why he did it this time. He wouldn't say. But he sounded pleased about something."

Pleased? That couldn't be a good sign. Especially since what might please Hyatt would almost certainly cause trouble for Ashley.

"Are you thinking what I'm thinking about that P.I. you hired to do a background check on Ashley?" Garrett asked.

Brayden nodded. "If he wasn't careful, Hyatt could have found Ashley by following him."

And that meant Brayden had led Hyatt right to her. Hell.

Of course, there was another alternative. That Trevor's Milquetoast demeanor was all an act. That he'd been the one to follow the P.I. and find Ashley. That Trevor had been the one to fire those shots.

"I want to talk to him." Brayden didn't wait for his

brother to respond. He started out of his office. "I want to find out what he really knows."

Garrett caught his arm. "Stating the obvious here, but I don't think that's wise."

"I don't think it's your decision to make." Brayden shook off his brother's grip and headed toward the interview room.

Garrett followed, as he'd known his brother would do. "If Trevor is the person trying to kill Ashley, we'll find out without you risking your badge."

Brayden tossed him a glare. "What the heck is that supposed to mean? I just want to ask him a few questions." But he knew exactly what Garrett meant.

"Yeah, and that fire in your eyes won't come into play when you're asking those questions, right?"

His brother's sarcasm set Brayden's teeth on edge. "I know how to interrogate a suspect, *Sergeant* O'Malley."

"You do, *Lieutenant* O'Malley. When you're objective. Which you aren't right now." Garrett latched onto him again just outside the interview room. "What's really going on here anyway?"

Brayden hitched a thumb to the door. "I'm trying to get in that room to ask Trevor Chapman some questions."

"Try answering my question first. Why the flash of temper? And don't say it's the shooting. I've seen how you react to being shot at, and, brother, this ain't it." Without more than a few seconds of hesitation,

Garrett's eyes widened. "It's Ashley. Are you falling for her?"

"No."

But it felt like a lie.

Worse, it sounded like one.

"This flash, as you call it, is just concern. *Concern* for her safety." Since his brother was now staring at him, Brayden added, "Tomorrow is the sixth day. Ashley should know if she's pregnant or not."

That didn't stop his brother from staring, even though it turned into somewhat of a flat look. "Are you falling for her?" Garrett repeated.

Brayden ignored him and went for a further explanation of why he was so damn agitated. "One way or another she'll leave. And I can't stop her. I'm afraid for her life."

"Are you falling for her?"

Brayden wanted to be thoroughly pissed off by his brother's repeated question. He wasn't. But that didn't stop him from going on the defensive. "I'm concerned about her. There's nothing wrong with that."

"No," Garrett quickly assured him. "And it wouldn't be wrong even if you fell in love with her."

Brayden felt as if he'd slugged him. "Say what?"

"You heard me. The way I see it, Ashley came through for Colton, for all of us. That makes her all right in my book."

Well, it made her all right in his book, too, but it

sure didn't make his feelings all right. "She's Dana's sister," Brayden pointed out.

"She's a good woman."

"She's off-limits!"

"Only because you put her there." Probably because they were starting to attract attention, Garrett thankfully lowered his voice. "Sheez, I'm not telling you to pop the frickin' question. All I'm saying is that it's okay for you to care for Ashley."

Brayden gave a troubled sigh. "Then why doesn't it feel okay, huh?"

Garrett didn't have time to answer. The interview-room door opened, and Brayden found himself face-to-face with Trevor Chapman. The moment obviously caught them both off guard. Brayden saw a glimpse of surprise in Trevor's attentive mud-brown eyes. Surprise and possibly something else.

Something that put Brayden's cop's instincts on full alert.

"Lieutenant," Trevor greeted.

Brayden shook his hand. Like the guy's forehead, it was sweaty. "Thank you for coming in today."

"I wanted to cooperate."

"Good. SAPD likes citizens who cooperate." And because he couldn't resist, because he just couldn't continue the nice-guy routine, Brayden added, "I wish your brother would do the same."

Trevor nodded. Not necessarily a nod of agree-

ment, though. "Hyatt feels w-w-wronged by the justice system."

"The majority of people in prison feel that way. I doubt their victims do, though. In fact, I'd imagine the man your brother beat within an inch of his life would think he's the one who'd been wronged by the justice system. After all, his attacker was a coward who ran rather than doing time."

Trevor's Milquetoast demeanor took a serious nosedive. Those brown eyes narrowed slightly. "If Hyatt calls again, I'll be sure to pass on your…sentiment."

Pleased that he'd finally gotten an honest reaction from the man, Brayden didn't stop there. "Pass this on to him as well—tell him I'd like to express my *sentiment* in person. Just the two of us. In fact, I'm looking forward to it."

Instead of the veiled threat Brayden expected as a comeback, Trevor looked past him. Well past him. Over Brayden's shoulder, in fact.

"Ashley?" Trevor said.

Brayden whipped around, dreading who he'd see.

Ashley was indeed there, and Katelyn had her by the arm. Ashley was resisting, but his sister was trying to pull her into one of the interview rooms, away from Trevor.

But it was too late.

Trevor saw her.

Ashley saw him. Worse, she moved out of Katelyn's grip and went toward him.

"Why are you here?" Brayden snarled. The last thing he wanted was for Trevor and Ashley to do a face-to-face.

Ashley didn't answer. She spared Brayden a glance and nailed her gaze to Trevor. "Are you the one who's trying to kill me?"

If Trevor had a reaction to that, he didn't show it. He simply leaned closer and dropped his voice to a secretive tone. "Is someone trying to kill you, Ashley?"

"It appears that way." She leaned closer, as well, despite Brayden's attempts to stop her. "I thought it might have something to do with what happened two and a half years ago. Some unresolved issues, perhaps? A little leftover venom?"

Trevor shrugged. "Why would there be venom?" But there was. Suddenly, his voice wasn't just whispered and secretive, it was bitter, a bitterness that made it all the way to his eyes. "Oh, unless I suspected that, instead of Dana and you working to get two acquittals, you cut a deal with the D.A. so Hyatt would go to jail."

"It wasn't a *deal* that convicted Hyatt. It was the evidence against him."

Trevor shrugged again.

When Ashley's expression turned to a scowl, Brayden knew he had to do something to get her out of there. He slipped his arm around her waist. "We have to talk *now*," he insisted.

Garrett did his part. He put his hand on Trevor's

back and got him moving in the opposite direction. But not before Ashley and Trevor exchanged arctic glares.

"Coming here wasn't a bright thing to do." Brayden pulled her into the interview room.

"Probably not. But if Trevor's the stalker, then he obviously already knew I was back in town. I just wanted to see how he'd react."

It sank in then. This wasn't an impromptu visit on Ashley's part. "Katelyn told you that Trevor and Miles Granville were coming into headquarters today?"

Ashley stepped away and avoided his gaze. "She might have mentioned it."

Great. He'd have a little talk with his sister about that later. "What if Trevor's the stalker, huh?" And to emphasize his point, he got right in her face. "What if your coming here allows him to find you?"

"Katelyn and I aren't going to advertise where I'm staying. We took precautions on the way over, and we'll take even more on the way back."

"You shouldn't have come," Brayden reiterated. "Seeing Trevor's reaction isn't worth risking your life."

"Well, Trevor's not exactly why I came. That was a perk, of sorts. I really wanted to talk to you."

"Nothing is so important that you should have risked coming here."

"I beg to differ." She reached in her purse, extracted a pen and handed it to him.

Except it wasn't a pen.

Brayden glanced down at the ocean-blue pen-shaped device. Specifically, at the tiny screen on it.

"We did it," Ashley whispered, pointing to the plus sign. "We really did it. I'm pregnant."

ASHLEY HADN'T BEEN SURE how Brayden would react to the fact that they were on their way to becoming parents. She'd braced herself for anything from jumps and shouts for joy to a tear-laced reckoning that they'd made it past the first step in saving Colton.

Neither of those things happened.

With his attention solely on that plus sign, Brayden nodded. "This is good news."

She'd gotten more jubilant reactions from her dentist for a good checkup. "Correct me if I'm wrong, but this is what you wanted, right?"

"Of course it is." He pulled his gaze from the test stick. "This baby is what we need, what I prayed for."

Okay. So they were on the same page.

Sort of.

Except Ashley was feeling a lot more jubilant, and there was no way she could contain it.

"I'm floating," she admitted, trying to keep her voice steady. She failed. "And the love is just unbelievable. I mean, I never thought it would feel like this. Never. But the love is automatic. Volumes and volumes of love for this tiny baby that didn't even exist a week ago."

Ashley was surprised and more than a little embarrassed when tears threatened. Here she was babbling like a hormone-infused idiot while Brayden just stood there—not babbling. In fact, not saying anything.

She blinked back the tears. "Okay, sorry about that. Gushing session over. I suspect you need some time to come to terms with what you're feeling right now."

She turned to leave, but only made it one step.

"I know what you mean about the love for the baby," Brayden said, his words slow and careful. "I feel it, too. And I feel the happiness. The floating."

Ashley turned back around and studied his face. "You don't exactly look like you're floating."

"It's a little tempered because I know this is just the beginning."

Yes. It was. And that was as good a lead-in as she would probably get.

"Dr. Ellison wants to see me tomorrow morning for a checkup." She'd intended to say it in one breath. Without hesitation. So that he'd know it didn't lack resolve. But Ashley didn't quite manage it. "After that, it's time for me to leave."

No shocked look, which meant he'd known what was coming. Part of her wanted to believe that was the real reason he hadn't jumped for joy about the positive pregnancy test, but it was a sad day in a woman's life when she toyed with the idea of lying to herself.

Brayden's less than enthusiastic response was no doubt because of Dana. Because this pregnancy reminded him of when Dana was pregnant with Colton. With *their* child. Brayden might never feel the same about this baby as he did about Colton. The idea of that bothered her far more than she'd ever thought it would.

"What about the amnio?" he asked.

"They can't do it for at least eight more weeks." Ashley paused to reinforce her voice so she could finish what she'd started. "And it doesn't have to be done here. I can have the test at a hospital in Houston."

Brayden's head whipped up. His gaze snared hers. "Why Houston?"

She shrugged. Then, shrugged again. "I thought I'd stay there until after the baby's born. And maybe even longer. Houston's not too far of a drive, so you'd be able to visit as often as you like."

"It might not be safe for you to go," he pointed out.

"It isn't safe for me to stay, either. I'll do what I did last time. Use an alias. Start a new life. Keep a low profile. I'll put my house up for sale here. I own it outright, and the market value's good, so there'll be no pressure for me to go back to work for a while."

His jaw muscles tightened. "You've given this a lot of thought."

She nodded. "Well, I've had a lot of time to think things through over the past five days."

"I know." He rubbed his fingers over his forehead and repeated it. "I'm sorry I haven't been there much."

"That wasn't a slam. Well, maybe it was a little one. And that brings me to what I really want you to hear. There's no reason for you to feel guilty about what happened between us. It was a necessity, and now there's just this weird intimacy because we made a baby together, that's all."

"You're not going to blame the kiss on primal instincts again?"

He'd asked it so casually, without changing his inflection, that it took Ashley a moment to realize he'd just zinged her.

"No. It was lust. Basic attraction," she readily admitted. "Hey, what can I say? You're cute, a good kisser, and you really get the juices flowing."

Brayden fought it. She could see him fight it. But he finally gave up and smiled. For a moment anyway. Before he obviously remembered the gist of this conversation.

Then he groaned. "What can I do to talk you out of leaving?"

"Nothing. Because it's the right thing to do. If I stay, Colton and you have no chance of a normal life. *None.* He wants to go home, Brayden. He needs normal. And that can't happen as long as I'm here."

His gaze came to hers again, and in his eyes she saw a lot of regret. "You're a brave woman."

It touched her that he'd think that about her. Even if it wasn't the truth. "No, I'm not. Bravery is for people who have a choice about what to do. Or so I've

been told. What I'm doing is just common sense. This way, we all stand a chance of being safe."

Ashley prayed that was true and not just lip service. Because there was a new player in this dangerous game.

Her baby.

And even though she'd only known about the baby for a couple of hours, it was more precious to her than her own life. She'd do whatever it took to protect it.

There was a soft knock at the door and a moment later, Garrett opened it. "Miles Granville is here."

Ashley instantly felt her heart rate kick up a notch. She'd known he was coming, of course. Katelyn had told her. Still, it renewed old concerns. Brought back old memories.

"I'll go with you to see him," Ashley insisted, hoping Brayden would automatically agree. "Just to say hello."

But Brayden didn't agree. He was already shaking his head before she finished her sentence. "It's too dangerous."

"Not really. We're at police headquarters. I'll have two, possibly three armed and dangerous O'Malleys with me. What do you say, Garrett?" she asked without looking back at him. "If it came down to it, would you protect me from Miles Granville?"

"Gladly," he assured her. "But I'm not the one you have to convince."

True. But Ashley knew Brayden's Achilles' heel. He was, after all, a cop. "I've known Miles since I was in high school. If he's the one who took shots at us, I don't think he'll be able to conceal it from me. All I want is to see him for a moment or two, and then I'll back off. You can take things from there."

"She might have a point," Garrett volunteered.

That earned him a scowl from Brayden.

"A quick hello," Ashley bargained before Brayden could do more than scowl. "With you and Garrett right there next to me."

Brayden hesitated. "What if Granville goes berserk? What if he comes after you right then, right there?"

"Then, it'd put an end to lots of our problems, wouldn't it? Because if he did that, then you'd know he was the stalker, the one who tried to kill us. Then, either you or Garrett would take him out."

Of course, even if Miles Granville was the stalker-gunman, Ashley didn't think he'd be stupid enough to attack her in police headquarters. And if she had thought that, for even a moment, she certainly wouldn't be risking Brayden's or her baby's life.

"You're sure you want to do this?" Brayden asked.

She nodded. "Absolutely."

Brayden grumbled something under his breath. Something about how he was sure he would regret this. It was punctuated with some profanity. But what he thankfully didn't do was try to stop her when Gar-

rett motioned for her to follow. Of course, Brayden followed, too.

Right next to her.

Garrett led them to the interview room at the end of the wide tiled hall. Ashley stepped in quickly, before Brayden could change his mind. Miles was there, near the wall, gazing into the two-way mirror that separated the interview and observation rooms.

Since his back was to her, Ashley took a moment to watch him. No expensive suit like Trevor's. Miles wore jeans, a plain white shirt and a nondescript blue jacket. Very low profile. Something she understood completely, especially since Miles had been in hiding, as well. Like her, he may have taken a risk just coming here.

"Miles," she greeted.

He turned. His eyes widened, and his head did a little bob as if he were doing a double take. Which he probably was.

"Ashley, is that you?" But he didn't wait for a confirmation. "Wow, it really is you. I didn't even recognize you. You changed your hair."

"You, too."

He no longer had a ponytail. His storm-black hair was now short and practical. But it wasn't the only change. When they'd dated, Miles had been on the lanky side. No longer. He'd bulked up considerably. Ashley understood that, too. She'd gone through fire-

arms training and self-defense classes, all in an effort to make her feel safe.

Smiling, Miles walked toward her, a gesture that caused both Brayden and Garrett to step in front of her.

His smile evaporated, and Miles gave her a puzzled look. "Is something wrong?"

Ashley pushed her way back through the two O'Malleys. "It's been a tense day," she remarked, studying his eyes. "How about you? How have you been?"

"Busy. I have a computer-security business that I operate out of my home. Keeps me working long hours."

Chitchat. Which should have put her at ease.

It didn't.

Because there shouldn't have been friendly chitchat between them.

The last time she'd seen Miles was at the courthouse, and he'd looked ready to tear her limb from limb because she was representing Hyatt. Of course, people did change, but Ashley wasn't ready to give her old boyfriend the benefit of the doubt.

"What about you?" Miles asked. "Are you still practicing law?"

"I'm taking a short sabbatical."

He made a sound of approval. His gaze slid over Garrett, over Brayden, and then back over her. His gaze paused a moment when it landed on Brayden's arm that was curved protectively around her waist.

Another sound. Definitely not of approval. "Well,

I didn't think I'd ever live to see the two of you together." Miles shook his head. "But it makes sense,
I guess. Funny though, I assumed neither of you
would be able to get past what happened to Dana."

"What do you mean?" Ashley asked at the same
moment Brayden insisted, "Think carefully before
you continue that thought, Granville."

And there it was.

That spark of fire and temper that she'd been looking for. It wasn't in Granville's eyes, but his smile.
Not exactly friendly. And that *not exactly friendly*
part was aimed at Brayden.

So, perhaps Miles was jealous.

That proved nothing, of course. It certainly didn't
mean he was a stalker and a killer.

However, it didn't mean he wasn't, either.

It only meant they still had three people on their
list of suspects. And they were no closer to finding
out which one of them wanted her dead.

HE WANTED HER DEAD.

Now.

But he had to choke back the rage and force himself not to act impulsively. After all, he wanted to walk
away from this when everything was said and done.
He wanted vengeance, but he could have that and his
freedom, too. This wasn't an *either-or* situation.

So now, the question was how?

Since O'Malley probably wouldn't let Ashley out

of his sight, that meant he'd have to die first. Probably a bullet to the head, which was sadly too quick. Much too painless. But removing O'Malley was his best bet for taking Ashley.

No bullet to the head for her. No. He was thinking something slow. Something he could savor for a while. And for that, he needed a private, quiet place where no one would interrupt them. He had just the place in mind.

Feeding off his anger, nursing it, he sat down to work out his plan of attack. By tomorrow, O'Malley would be dead, and Ashley would be his.

All his.

Well, until he killed her, that is.

Chapter Thirteen

"Stay low in the seat," Brayden warned.

Ashley tried to get a peek out the side mirror, but he simply put his hand on her shoulder and pushed her back down. The only thing she caught a glimpse of was a huge fake Christmas tree in front of an office building. "Why, do you see someone suspicious?"

"No. But if I do, I don't want that person to see you, as well."

She agreed with that. However, it'd made for an uncomfortable, tense drive. The drive to Dr. Ellison's clinic for the appointment that would normally have taken ten minutes or so had become an hour-plus adventure. First, they'd driven to headquarters and changed cars. Then they'd driven to the county sheriff's office and switched cars a second time. Finally, Brayden had driven around the city, making every turn seemingly possible so he could be certain no one was following them. It was a lot of precautions.

Unfortunately, they were necessary.

"I really wish you'd reconsider this," Brayden mumbled. Again.

Ashley didn't have to ask what *this* was. She knew. It'd been Brayden's choice of subject since they'd started this meandering trip, and it didn't have anything to do with the doctor's appointment. He was trying yet again to talk her out of leaving.

"We've got Trevor and Miles under surveillance," he reiterated. "If they make one wrong move, we can arrest them. Then if you still want to go to Houston, it'd be safe."

"But it might be years—or never—before Trevor or Miles makes a wrong move."

It was the *never* part that Ashley prayed for and yet wished it would come, just so it'd be over. Running was getting tiresome, and it likely wouldn't get easier now that she was pregnant.

She ran her hand over her stomach, and despite the dire thoughts, Ashley smiled.

A baby.

The change in her was already incredible, even though she'd only known about the baby for twenty-four hours. Two weeks ago, she hadn't even considered having a child, and now here she was. Pregnant. By Brayden. And extremely happy about it.

Who would have thought it possible?

"Are you okay?" he asked.

Ashley followed his gaze to see what had prompted his question. It was her hand on her stom-

ach. "I'm fine. Really," she added when he gave her a skeptical glance. "Okay, better than fine. Excited."

He pulled into the parking lot, and he immediately began to check it out. Like the rest of the drive, Ashley didn't see much. Only the dull gray sky and the cheery wreaths high on the metal light poles.

"Since you're not a novice at this pregnancy stuff, it's probably not as exciting for you," she continued when he didn't answer.

"It's exciting. Never doubt that. I want this baby as much as you do. And not just because of Colton."

Ashley waited a moment to see if Brayden was finished. He apparently was. "Do I detect a *but* at the end of that?"

He drew in a heavy breath. "You know I'm worried."

Yes, but that covered a lot of territory. "Worried as in guilty worried because of Dana, or worried as in worried worried because of the stalker?"

"Both," he readily answered.

Again she waited, but Brayden didn't add anything. Not surprising. Their conversations usually came to a halt when Dana's name was mentioned. "It's ironic. We're the two people who loved Dana more than anyone else, and yet we can't even talk about her."

Silence again. Brayden pulled into a parking space, directly beneath one of those wreaths. He took off his seat belt and opened his coat, probably so he'd have easier access to the gun he had in his shoulder holster.

"We'll wait here for a couple of minutes," he informed her. "I have an officer inside the clinic, checking out the corridors and the doctor's office. Once he gives us the okay, we'll go in."

She nodded. And sighed. Once again, they'd skirted the issue of Dana.

Or so she thought.

"I believe Dana would have approved of what we're doing," Brayden said, his voice practically a whisper. "Because we're trying to help Colton."

"Yes." And she kept her response at that. A safe response. In case that was as deep into the conversation as Brayden wanted to get.

It apparently wasn't.

"But I think Dana would have approved for others reasons, too," Brayden continued. He gave a soft, frustrated groan. "She definitely wouldn't have wanted us punishing ourselves, the way we've been doing."

"No. I suspect not."

Brayden glanced down at her. "'So you found out, huh?'"

It took Ashley a moment to realize he wasn't asking her a confusing question but rather repeating what she'd said to him that day he'd arrived in Virginia.

Mercy.

She didn't want to get into that now, maybe not ever. Why had she let it slip?

"Judging from that deer-in-the-headlights look in

your eyes, it's not good," he mumbled. "I didn't think it would be. Or you would have already told me."

Ashley tried to change that look in her eyes, but Brayden was giving her his own *look*. One that told her he wouldn't back down on this. Not this time.

"Was Dana having an affair?" Brayden asked. But despite Ashley frantically shaking her head, he didn't wait for an answer. "Because I won't believe that. *Ever.* I don't care what kind of proof you think you have."

"It was nothing like that, Brayden. I promise you Dana never would have cheated on you. She loved you."

There was no relief in his eyes. "Then what was it? What was so bad that you had to keep it a secret all this time?"

"It's not bad." Well, not bad depending on perspective. From her perspective, it hadn't been good. And the consequences had been deadly. "Heck, it's not even important. Not anymore."

"Not important, huh? Then, there's absolutely no reason for you not to tell me."

Oh, there were reasons. Old hurts. Old wounds. Old issues. Old everything.

"Whatever it is," he continued. "Don't you think I have a right to know?"

He did. That wouldn't make it palatable. But at least now they were discussing Dana. A rarity. And a necessity. They somehow needed to get past this

and move on. Maybe it was truly time for that air clearing she'd wanted.

"Dana knew," Ashley said. Not with much conviction. But she moistened her lips and forced herself to continue. "She knew the Chapmans were guilty of trying to murder Miles Granville."

That brought his gaze rifling to hers. "What do you mean she knew?" Not a simple question. Nor was it mild surprise. Brayden's voice had an accusing tone to it.

Well, what had she expected? This would not be welcome news. So much for air clearing.

"Trevor confessed everything to her," Ashley explained, choosing her words carefully. "I read it in her computer notes when I was cleaning out her office."

"She knew?" Brayden shook his head. "I can't believe she knew."

Rather than look at him while she continued, Ashley stared at her purse. "I suspect she didn't tell either of us because of client confidentiality. And because she was concerned that I wouldn't have taken the case if I'd known."

Brayden cursed. Not polite cursing. And the accusatory tone was back. "Please don't tell me you're blaming Dana for her own death?"

"No! Absolutely not." Ashley tried to get up, but he pushed her back down again. "Sheez. I knew this would happen. I'm simply informing you of what I found. You asked, remember?"

"I remember." And that was all he said for several moments. "Are you telling me that you wouldn't have defended Chapman if you'd known he was guilty?"

"Is that such a huge surprise?" Ashley noted his narrow-eyed, stern expression. "Yes. I guess it is. Well, here's another surprise. I didn't want to defend Hyatt Chapman at all. In addition to Hyatt being a bona fide jackass, I knew that by defending him, I'd alienate Miles and ruin any hope of restoring our friendship."

"And that mattered to you?" Again, asked with tons of negative insinuations.

"At the time, yes it did. A lot. Miles and I had been dating for over a year. We were friends in addition to being lovers, and even though the lover part was a mistake, I didn't want to lose our friendship."

"If you knew Hyatt was a jackass, then why didn't you tell Dana about the psych eval?"

Ashley groaned. She'd almost forgotten what it was like to be on the receiving end of one of Brayden's interrogations.

"Well?" he prompted. Except it was a little more than a prompt.

"All right, here goes. I didn't tell Dana because Hyatt threatened to sue me if I released that info to anyone. It was a personal evaluation, one I'd requested. One *he* paid for since he was the client. I'm sure he wanted to keep it secret since it was a lot more

revealing than the assessment done by the D.A.'s shrink."

"Yeah. Because Hyatt probably lied on that one," Brayden mumbled.

"He probably did. And if it helps, I blame myself for not realizing that."

"And you blame Dana for not telling you the Chapmans were guilty."

"Stop putting words in my mouth," Ashley warned. "No. I don't blame her. I've never blamed her, even after I read her computer notes. I should have known they were guilty. I should have known that taking the case would cause problems. If I could, I'd go back and undo it." She cursed. "And we're right back to square one again."

The silence closed in around them.

Forcing herself to calm down, Ashley ran her hand over her stomach. Over her baby. It helped. Not completely. But it diffused enough of her anger so that she could speak.

"Two and a half years ago when we had this argument, we said some really hurtful things to each other. Let's do us both a favor and not repeat them, okay? In fact, let's just end this conversation right now. In an hour or two I'll be on my way to Houston. We won't have to put ourselves through this again. Promise."

"I don't want a promise."

It sounded a little like an apology. Maybe. But be-

fore her eyes could meet his, something else caught her attention. Something on the driver's side of the car. A flash of movement.

A person in a Santa suit.

Brayden must have detected something, as well, because he turned, reaching for his weapon in the same motion.

But it was already too late.

A silenced bullet slammed through the window, webbing the glass and obstructing the view of their attacker. The car door flew open.

Brayden had his hand on his gun, halfway drawn. But halfway wasn't enough. Because the man in the Santa suit latched onto Brayden's shoulder. Where there was blood.

God, there was blood.

Before Ashley could release her seat belt, the man pressed a club against Brayden's back. But not just a club. A stun gun. The jolt fired through Brayden. His muscles jerked, spasmed, incapacitating him almost instantly. The man dragged him out of the car and threw him down to the pavement.

And reaimed his gun.

Right at Brayden's head.

"No!" Ashley screamed.

She launched herself across the seat, fighting her way through the narrow space past the gearshift and steering wheel. She grabbed the man's wrist. Wrenching his hand away from Brayden. In the scuf-

fle, his fake white beard dropped down. And she saw his face.

She saw Hyatt Chapman.

"Don't, Hyatt!" she yelled, still gripping his wrist and the weapon. Ashley didn't let go.

She brought up her knee, prepared to ram it into Hyatt's groin, but she never got the chance. She never saw the stun gun coming at her.

But she felt it.

The staticky shock shot through her. Overpowered her. Until her limbs went limp. Until she couldn't move.

Until the world turned blurry and gray.

She was powerless to stop Hyatt when he gathered her up and tossed her back into the car. Unable to escape. Unable to help Brayden.

Helpless, she slumped against the seat. Ashley thought of her unborn baby. Of Brayden and Colton.

And how she might never see either of them again.

THE FEELING IN HIS ARMS AND LEGS came back slowly. Too slowly. Brayden couldn't say the same for his mind. It was racing. Yelling for him to get up off the ground and go after Ashley.

Hyatt Chapman had Ashley.

The bastard had her.

The officer who rushed to the scene was busy calling for backup. There was a doctor applying pressure to Brayden's shoulder wound and insisting that the

stretcher would be there in just a second or two to carry him inside the clinic.

Brayden knew for a fact that wasn't going to happen.

"Lieutenant O'Malley, can you hear me?" the officer asked.

He managed a nod and sucked in enough breath so he could speak. "Get my brother. And Trevor Chapman's address."

"Sir, you need medical attention," he said as if stating the obvious.

"My brother," Brayden ordered. "And Chapman's address. *Now.*"

The cop nodded, probably too afraid to disobey.

Brayden lay there, listening to the sound of sirens, forcing the feeling back into his arms and legs. Eventually, he was able to sit up.

"I wouldn't advise that," the doctor insisted.

Brayden did it anyway.

"Your brother's on the way," the officer relayed. He handed Brayden a scrap of paper with a scrawled address. "Trevor Chapman's residence and his business address."

"Call both. Don't identify yourself and then hang up. When you find out where he is, get a unit over there to make sure he stays put. Do it!" Brayden demanded when the cop hesitated.

Brayden caught onto the doctor and used the man's arm to hoist himself up. He gave his injury a

cursory check. The bullet had skimmed across the top of his left shoulder. Definitely not life threatening.

Unlike what Ashley was no doubt going through. Hell.

If Hyatt hurt her…but Brayden wouldn't think beyond that. Somehow, he had to get to her.

He had to save her.

Because this wasn't just about Colton and the baby she carried. This was about Ashley.

"Trevor Chapman's at his residence," the officer informed him.

"Get me a car."

Again, the officer shook his head. The doctor balked, as well. Brayden ignored both of them and would have commandeered a vehicle, any vehicle, if Garrett and his black Mustang hadn't come to a screeching halt in front of him.

His brother asked no questions. Instead, Garrett leaned over and opened the door for him. Brayden got inside, and they sped away.

Brayden handed him the slip of paper with Trevor's address. "Get there. Fast."

Garrett glanced at the address and gunned the engine. "We can make it in under ten minutes."

Brayden called Katelyn, to make sure she was with Colton. She was. Thank heaven. And she hadn't seen Hyatt. It didn't mean that the man wouldn't go there. Brayden's next call was to his brother-in-law, Joe, so that he could provide backup for Katelyn if necessary.

"I heard the report," Garrett explained, weaving in between some cars. He was definitely speeding, but Brayden was thankful for it. "You're sure it was Hyatt who took Ashley?"

"Positive. I doubt he'll go to his brother's house, but I'm guessing Trevor will know where he is."

"Might be fun getting Trevor to turn into a chatterbox." Garrett tipped his head to the blood on Brayden's coat. "How bad are you hurt?"

"It looks worse than it is."

"Good. Because it looks like you're wearing about a half pint of A-Positive." Garrett paused long enough to take a curve on what had to be two wheels. "Did Hyatt hurt Ashley?"

Before he could answer, Brayden had to push aside some gut-wrenching images. Images of her fighting for his life, and hers, in the parking lot. "He hit her with the stun gun, but he didn't shoot her."

At least, Hyatt hadn't done that in the parking lot. Hell, he could have done anything to her afterward. It'd been fifteen minutes, maybe twenty. That was a lifetime for a criminal to carry a victim to a secondary crime scene.

"Don't go there," Garrett warned. "Keep those negative thoughts out of your head because I need you fully functioning here."

"Oh, I'm functioning all right. Full throttle."

"Well, you might want to lighten up on that throttle some. And remember, if this requires a little mus-

cle, that's where I come in. I don't want you losing your badge over this."

"What about *your* badge?" Brayden countered.

Garrett dismissed that with a shrug. "People expect me to act like a thug. It's my whole badass, *Lethal Weapon* image. You, on the other hand, are not badass material. Not even close."

Wrong. He was. Well, he was where Ashley and his baby were concerned. His body was practically begging for a fight.

Garrett pulled to a loud stop in front of Trevor Chapman's house, and they both barreled out of the car. The noise must have alerted Trevor because he opened his front door and stepped onto the porch.

"What's this—"

That was as much as Trevor got out. Garrett hooked his arm around the man and shoved him inside.

"Where's Hyatt?" Brayden demanded, shutting the door behind them.

"I don't think I like your tone." He slung off Garrett's grip. "And I know I don't like being manhandled."

"Where's Hyatt!" Brayden repeated.

And it wasn't a request.

Maybe it was the brutal tone or Garrett's menacing scowl, but fear crept into Trevor's eyes. "I don't know where he is. What happened?"

Brayden wasn't even sure he could say the words, but somehow he got them out. "He kidnapped Ashley."

No outraged gasp or look of stunned surprise. But

there was something. Some heated emotion. Nothing wussy. Nothing light. This emotion was deep, and Brayden thought the man might actually be angry.

"Did you tell him that you saw Ashley at headquarters?" Brayden demanded.

"I might have mentioned it."

Garrett latched onto a handful of Trevor's shirt and slammed his back against the wall. "Anything else you might have mentioned to Hyatt?"

"Maybe. Maybe I said something about her having a doctor's appointment today." With his eyes dark, he looked at Brayden. "I overheard Ashley and you talking when you were in the interview room."

It took every ounce of Brayden's self-control not to launch himself at the man. Trevor might not have been the one to kidnap Ashley, but he'd damn well given his brother the information necessary to do it.

Brayden took a step closer until he was right in Trevor's face. It took a moment to unclench his teeth so he could speak. "Now, let's try this again. Where's Hyatt?"

"I told you I don't know. And this is police harassment." His eyes narrowed. "I expected better from SAPD's leading Boy Scout. Does the Chief know you're here, Lieutenant?"

Garrett tightened the grip he had on Trevor's shirt and did another body slam into the wall. It rattled some nearby paintings. "If you don't tell us where your scum-ball brother is, it'll be more than just har-

assment. Hyatt shot a cop and tried to kill him. You said it yourself—Brayden's the Boy Scout of the department. But guess what? I'm not."

Trevor volleyed uneasy glances at both of them. What Brayden didn't see was that click of fear and desperation. That look of absolute panic to indicate that Trevor believed he might not live through this.

Tired of wasting time, Brayden pulled out his weapon, the metal rasping against his leather holster. He put his gun to Trevor's head. Hard. So that it dug into his skin.

"Talk," Brayden demanded.

The click of fear happened almost immediately, as Brayden figured it would. He saw it in Trevor's eyes. The man gave an awkward nod. "He rented a house on Natchitoches Road. Just outside the city limits."

"Be more specific," Brayden insisted.

"It's a couple of miles from the race track. It's not easy to get to, lots of turns, and I'm not even sure if he's there. He didn't let me in on his plans."

Brayden reholstered his gun. "Stay here with him," he told Garrett. "Make sure he doesn't try to warn his brother."

Garrett nodded. "Please tell me you're not going out there alone?"

He was. There was no other choice. "Call for silent backup. No one moves in unless I order it. Trevor here will provide you with directions—*accurate* di-

rections—to Hyatt's house. Call me when you have them, but I want to get a head start. I also want side roads or any other access route I can use to get to this house."

Brayden started for the door, adding his last instruction from over his shoulder. "If Trevor refuses to cooperate, I'll be back to beat the information out of him."

And in his state of mind, that wasn't a bluff.

Chapter Fourteen

"Bet you were surprised to see me today, huh?" Hyatt taunted. "Ho, ho, ho."

Ashley ignored him. Just as she'd ignored the other caustic remarks he'd tossed at her over the past forty-five minutes. She'd ignored him and remained quiet. Trying not to react, trying not to move a muscle. Even though she was almost positive she could move now.

Best to let him think she was still incapacitated.

She carefully watched where he was driving. Committing each turn to memory. He'd backtracked a couple of times, probably to make sure they weren't being followed, and now they were out of the city limits on a two-lane road with rolling hills and thick trees.

And virtually no other traffic or houses.

Since Hyatt was speeding, at least seventy miles an hour, that made it impossible for her to jump out of the car. But eventually he'd have to slow down. Or stop. And that's when she would make her move. Be-

cause somehow she had to get away, and she'd need to find her way back to the main highway when that happened.

And it would happen.

It *had* to happen. She couldn't die. Not here. Not like this. Because if so, her baby would die, too. And maybe even Colton.

Maybe Brayden was already dead.

After all, Hyatt had shot him. There'd been blood. She'd seen the blood.

Ashley couldn't help it. That brought on the tears, and she choked back a sob. Crying definitely wouldn't help. Right now, she had to concentrate on escaping. Then, she could make sure Brayden was all right.

"I'd just about given up hope of finding you," Hyatt commented in a discussing-the-weather tone. "Well, maybe given up isn't the right word. I would never have given up. Old scores have to be settled."

Yes. She knew about old scores. Hyatt had killed Dana. He'd hurt Brayden. One way or another, he'd pay for both. She would see to it.

Hyatt slowed, shoving his foot hard against the brakes. Ashley fastened her attention on the turn just ahead. A sharp turn. Which would no doubt require him to slow down even more. She inched her hand toward the door handle.

So she'd be ready.

The moment he made the turn, she'd bolt out of the car and start running. The woods were close to

the road and thick enough that she might be able to make it behind some trees before he fired at her.

Might.

It wasn't a guarantee, but then nothing was at this point. Too bad he'd tossed her purse into the back seat. Not only was her phone in there, but she had some pepper spray, as well. Either would have come in handy.

Hyatt approached the turn, slowing down even more. Ashley moved her hand closer to the handle. She adjusted her feet slightly so she could barrel out.

"Don't even think about it," Hyatt said. He followed up that threat by whipping out the gun from the jacket of his Santa suit. He aimed it right at her.

Ashley mentally cursed.

So much for her ruse of not being able to move.

"I figure you got the feeling back in your arms and legs at least a half hour ago," Hyatt explained. "The stun gun wasn't that powerful. Only about 70,000 volts. Definitely not strong enough to do any permanent damage. Just enough to restrain you for a little while."

Even though that might be a lie, Ashley clung to that. Maybe the jolt hadn't hurt her baby.

Without lowering his gun, Hyatt made the turn. And Ashley watched her escape plan fade away.

"I have other things in mind for you," Hyatt went on. "Like for starters, a discussion. We'll rehash old times, specifically the trial."

"And then you'll kill me."

He shrugged. "Perhaps."

There was no perhaps to it. Hyatt was obviously insane. He'd shot a cop in broad daylight and then kidnapped her. Definitely not the actions of a reasonable man. It was her guess that he planned to torture her, kill her and then go back on the run.

"Why did you kill Dana?" Ashley asked. Not that she expected an answer. And she certainly didn't expect the question to help dissolve the obvious hatred he had for her. "I was your lawyer, not her. She had nothing to do with you being sentenced for a crime you committed."

For the first time since they'd begun this nightmarish trip, she saw something hesitant in his body language. Definitely not the cocky demeanor he'd had so far.

Hyatt shook his head. "I didn't kill her."

Almost certainly a lie.

"Actually, Dana was okay, even if she was married to a cop," he continued. "She got Trevor off with just parole. Gotta admire that about her."

That *okay* part didn't mean Hyatt hadn't shot Dana by mistake. Maybe he'd expected her and not Dana to step out of that car.

"Parole," Hyatt repeated. "Nice ending to that story, huh? But mine wasn't so nice, thanks to you and your little chat with the D.A."

"That chat was routine, and he came to me, not the other way around. I didn't bargain."

"I don't believe you. You got me a felony conviction. Five years in jail—"

"Not a harsh sentence for attempted murder."

"You see, that's where we disagree. It was harsh all right because it caused the board of directors to oust me as CEO of the family business. Not that I blame them. After all, they couldn't have their CEO out of commission for five years while doing time. Hardly conducive to good business."

"Hardly," Ashley mumbled sarcastically.

He laughed. "Love your sense of humor. Always have. But that particular love won't get you off the hook, darling. Because the person I blame for all of this is you."

"Is that so?"

"I should never have been tried for attempted murder. If I'd attempted to kill Miles, he'd be rotting in the ground right now. And I wouldn't have chosen to do it with my fists, either. I simply wanted to express my disappointment at the way he backstabbed Trevor and me on that business deal."

"I think you got your point across. He was in a coma for two days and had twenty-three stitches."

"Yeah. I made my point." Another chuckle. "Old score settled."

Was it really? Or perhaps a more reasonable explanation was that Hyatt hadn't been able to find Miles so he could finish the job. After all, Miles had been in hiding, too. That had probably saved them both.

Until now, that is.

"Of course, now I have another little problem." With the gun still in his hand, Hyatt gave the rear-view mirror an adjustment. "If O'Malley's alive, I think he might know that I'm the one who took you. I'd hoped for incognito status, but once again I have you to thank for screwing up my life."

Hyatt made yet another turn. This time, down a narrow country road. He drove to the end, less than a mile, and brought the car to a stop in front of a mod-est one-story brick house. Ashley knew if he was able to get her inside, her chances of survival would decrease significantly.

But then, her chances weren't very good if she made a run for it.

Not with that gun still aimed at her.

Without taking his gaze off her, Hyatt opened his car door and planted one foot on the ground. "Let's go over the rules so there's no misunderstanding. You'll get out, without trying to escape or do any-thing else to upset me, and then you'll walk into the house. Because you see, even though it's not my first choice of how things should happen, I *will* shoot you, Ashley. Understand?"

She nodded. Not that her nod was a compliance. Because she fully intended to do something, and it would almost certainly *upset* him.

"Open your door," he instructed, walking around the front of the car toward her.

She did. Slowly. Her muscles felt unsteady, probably a leftover effect of the stun gun, but she forced
herself to move, to concentrate. Thankfully, the chilly
winter air helped. The wind gusted against her face.

Ashley glanced around. There was a cluster of
oaks on the right side of the house. Unfortunately,
they were at least twenty yards away.

Too far.

Hyatt would easily get off a shot if she tried to
run there.

Behind her, also to her right, there was an old-
fashioned well. One made of stone and mortar and
topped with a crumbling wooden roof. It wasn't very
wide, but if she could get to it, it would at least provide her with some protection.

Temporary protection.

Under the circumstances, that was the most she
could hope for.

Ashley stepped out of the car. Again, slowly.
While she checked the ground around her feet. It
was littered with limestone rocks. Some were small
enough that she'd be able to lift them. She mentally
chose the one closest to her right hand and came up
with a plan.

A risky plan.

She'd drop down, grab the rock, and when Hyatt
rushed around to her side of the car, she would hit
him with it. After that, she'd get behind the well and
then do whatever it took to get away.

Whatever it took could encompass a lot.

Ashley left the car door open, in case she had to use it for cover. And she prepared herself for the fight.

"On the count of three," she mumbled to herself.

"Get moving," Hyatt ordered.

One.

Two.

And she saw the movement. The shadowy figure in the trees to her right.

Brayden.

Mercy, it was Brayden. Alive.

Relief flooded through her.

But for only a split second.

Because Hyatt must have seen the movement, too. He turned toward Brayden and fired.

BRAYDEN DROPPED to the ground, praying that Ashley would do the same. Praying that she could somehow get herself out of Hyatt's line of fire.

She did.

Ashley grabbed a chunk of limestone and took cover behind the car door. It wasn't enough. Not nearly enough because Hyatt lunged across the hood toward her.

Brayden fired. And cursed when Hyatt rolled to the side just in time to avoid being hit. The man dropped down onto the other side of the car. Away from Ashley. But also away from Brayden's bullets.

Brayden hadn't wanted it to come down to this,

and he certainly hadn't intended for Hyatt to spot him so soon. He'd wanted to get Ashley out of the way first. Perhaps give her a signal to drop down, so he'd be able to get in a better position and have a cleaner shot at Hyatt.

But that hadn't happened.

Now, Ashley was in more danger than she had been just moments earlier.

Hell.

Fearing that Hyatt would shoot her from beneath the car, Brayden came out of cover again. A lure. To draw Hyatt's attention to him.

"Chapman, throw down your weapon and surrender," Brayden yelled.

Not that he expected Hyatt Chapman to do that any time soon. But he wanted the man's focus away from Ashley.

It worked.

Instead of firing beneath the car, Hyatt popped up, fired at Brayden, and ducked right back down again.

Brayden did some ducking of his own, throwing himself back to the ground. Thankfully so did Ashley. Keeping low, she scrambled toward the well and dived behind it. All things considered, it was probably the best spot in the yard for her. But with Hyatt so close, it still wasn't safe.

While keeping his weapon aimed and ready to fire, Brayden inched closer and peered through a patch of dried weeds. He could see the car, easily.

And he could see Ashley. She was pressed against the well with rocks in each hand. But he couldn't tell where Hyatt was. He certainly didn't want the man racing around the back of the car to get to Ashley. If so, she'd be trapped, with no place to run or hide.

That couldn't happen.

"Other officers are already on the way," Brayden informed Hyatt, hoping it would cause the man to fire again. "You can't escape."

Hyatt stayed put. "Wanta make a bet? The cops haven't been able to find me in two and a half years."

"I found you," he pointed out.

"Blind luck."

"No luck involved. Your brother told me exactly where you were." Brayden crawled forward. "Trevor was very cooperative. In fact, so cooperative that I'm thinking about giving him a good citizenship award or something."

Silence.

Dead silence.

Maybe Hyatt was seething about his brother's possible betrayal. If so, that anger might cause him to make a mistake.

"Did you hurt Trevor?" Hyatt demanded.

Brayden inched closer before he answered. "I didn't have to. He got scared and talked. He doesn't want to be an accessory to another felony."

"Liar!" Hyatt's voice was still resounding through the air when he darted out of cover and fired.

The shot came close. Too close. It smashed into the weeds just to the right of Brayden's head. However, the close call gave him exactly the information he needed. Hyatt was on the side of the driver's door.

Brayden took aim, not at the car, but at the narrow space below it and returned fire.

And then all hell broke loose.

Brayden had only a split second to react. Firing wildly, not with one weapon but two, Hyatt rushed around the back of the car. Headed right toward Ashley.

She must have heard him coming because she went into a defensive posture, bringing up the rocks. But Brayden knew those rocks wouldn't protect her if Hyatt fired at her.

He had to stop Hyatt from doing that.

Brayden came out of cover. Just as Hyatt launched himself away from the car and dived toward the well. Ashley didn't stay down.

Damn it.

She came up and pelted Hyatt with one of the rocks. It knocked one of the guns from his hand, but he simply turned the other one on her.

Brayden didn't shoot to stop Hyatt. He shot to kill. A double tap of the trigger. The bullets blasted through the air and slammed into the man who was only seconds away from shooting Ashley.

The impact of the bullets in his chest stopped Hyatt.

Hyatt's startled gaze rifled to Brayden, and even

though he was already slumping toward the ground, he took aim at Brayden. Brayden dived to the side and, in the same motion, fired a third shot.

Hyatt smiled an eerie, sickening smile and dropped face first to the driveway. Unfortunately, his gun stayed firmly planted in his right hand.

"Stay put, Ashley," Brayden called out to her.

He didn't want to take a chance that Hyatt was still alive and just waiting for an opportunity to kill them.

Keeping low, and with his weapon still ready to fire, Brayden made his way through the thick underbrush and trees. He approached Hyatt cautiously, bracing himself in case the man turned over. When Brayden was close enough, he kicked the gun from Hyatt's hand.

No reaction.

So he leaned down and pressed his fingers to the man's neck.

"He's dead," Brayden let Ashley know.

Brayden went to her, keeping her on the far side of the well so she wouldn't have to see Hyatt's bullet-riddled body. "Are you all right? Did he hurt you?"

"I'm okay. I'm okay." Her gaze landed on the blood on his coat. "But you're not."

"It's nothing serious."

She shook her head. "You're sure?"

"Positive. And Hyatt won't be bothering anyone else ever again."

Despite his attempt to stop her from seeing Hyatt,

Ashley looked over his shoulder at the man lying on the ground.

"It's really over?" she asked, her voice crumbling.

"It's really over."

Brayden gathered her into his arms and didn't let go.

Chapter Fifteen

Ashley checked her watch and paced the living room in Brayden's house. Why, she didn't know. Pacing and checking the time certainly didn't help.

Nothing had so far.

Not the shower she'd taken.

Or the nap, which she hadn't really taken but had told Katelyn she had.

Or the calls she'd made so she could start arranging a real Christmas for Colton. A Christmas with a tree, bags of fake snow and those twenty gifts she'd promised him. All of which should be delivered within the next twenty-four hours.

But none of those things had soothed her. None could. Because she didn't stand a chance of relaxing until she saw Brayden. She had to know if he was all right. The image of the blood on his jacket was still much too vivid for her not to worry.

"Still wound up a little?" Katelyn asked in between bites of a sandwich. Not a real question but ob-

viously a rhetorical, semisarcastic one. Katelyn added a wink to it.

Another check of Ashley's watch. "You know, I really appreciate you staying here with me until Brayden gets back, but it's not necessary. I'm sure you'd rather be spending this time with your husband."

Katelyn nodded. "I'd rather be with Joe. I admit it. But you're wrong about it not being necessary for me to be here. It is. Because we both know you really shouldn't be alone right now."

That was partly true. All right, it was completely true. Ashley didn't want to be alone. Because it'd only been ten hours since Brayden had shot and killed Hyatt. Ten short, grueling hours. The memories were still much too fresh.

"Why don't you sit down and have another cup of chamomile tea?" Katelyn asked.

"Because the first three cups didn't help." Ashley made an agitated sound when another jolt of nervous energy knifed through her. "You'd think I'd be exhausted by now. What with the reports at headquarters and the adrenaline crash and burn."

"You haven't crashed and burned yet. That'll happen later tonight."

"Great. Something to look forward to." More pacing. Another check of her watch. "What's taking Brayden so long?"

"Reams of paperwork. Interviews, reinterviews.

You name it. There are checks and double checks when something like this happens."

Because he'd killed someone. In the line of duty, of course. But that didn't absolve him of having to explain why he'd used deadly force. Her own interview had likely been easy compared to his.

"Certainly the captain or someone would have forced Brayden to get medical attention?" Ashley mumbled.

Katelyn shrugged. "Probably."

But she didn't say it with enough conviction. Which meant he might not have seen a doctor yet. Well, she would remedy that as soon possible.

As soon as possible came soon.

Ashley heard the garage open, and she went sprinting down the hall toward the door. Katelyn did some sprinting of her own. And for the first time in two and a half years, the racing and hurrying didn't have to do with the fear that she'd be facing a stalker. Thanks to Brayden, she wouldn't have to worry about that again.

Ashley and Brayden opened the door at the same time. Their gazes met, and she saw the stark weariness in his eyes.

It was a challenge to stop herself from grabbing hold of him. If she did, she might not let go. She might hang on to the security that only his arms could give her. And Brayden didn't look as if he should be on the giving end of such comfort. So, Ashley stayed

back and settled for gently touching his arm with her fingertips.

"How'd it go at headquarters?" Katelyn asked.

Thankfully, she asked it. Because Ashley's throat clamped shut so that she couldn't ask anything. It was good to see him. So good to have him close again.

Mercy, her heart was racing.

"Everything went as expected," Brayden answered. "Well, almost. Trevor Chapman's attorney will probably file harassment charges against me."

Ashley groaned. "That little weasel. I'll talk to him. I'll get him to change his mind."

"No. You won't," Brayden insisted. "I don't want you anywhere near Trevor. We're looking into filing charges against him as an accessory to your kidnapping."

Then, Trevor was a battle she'd save for another time, but Ashley didn't intend to let him come after Brayden with these legal threats. Especially since any potential harassment would have no doubt been done so Brayden could find her.

Besides, she had other battles to fight right now, and the most obvious one was the injury that had caused the bloodstain on his clothes. "How's your shoulder?"

"Fine. How about you? Are you okay?"

She nodded. And it wasn't exactly a lie, either. Now, that Brayden was there, she felt as close to being okay as she had in years.

"I took Ashley to the doctor," Katelyn volunteered. "Clean bill of health. The doc said the stun gun wouldn't have caused any damage."

The worry lines on his forehead relaxed a little. Until he glanced down at his coat. Specifically at the dried patch of blood. "I need to grab a shower, change my clothes, and then I can drop by Mom and Dad's and get Colton."

"I have a better idea." Katelyn took out her phone. "Let Colton stay put for the night. They're decorating the tree anyway. And that means you can get some rest. I'll pick him up in the morning and bring him home."

Ashley expected Brayden to argue, to insist that he see Colton tonight, but instead he gave a tired nod and kissed his sister on the cheek. "Thanks." He turned his gaze to Ashley. "You'll be here when I get out of the shower?"

"Sure." And Ashley watched him disappear into his bathroom. Moments later, she heard him turn on the water. "You think he'll be all right?" she asked Katelyn.

"It might take a day or two. My guess is he feels guilty for letting Hyatt get to you."

Ashley's mouth dropped open. "That's ridiculous. Brayden couldn't have prevented that."

"Really?" Katelyn stretched out the syllables. "So, you don't feel guilty for letting Hyatt get to Brayden?"

Of course she did.

And Katelyn knew that.

That's why she gave Ashley a friendly little smirk and an equally friendly pat on the stomach. "Take good care of my niece. And it will be a girl because the O'Malleys are already under a thick cloud of testosterone. We need another female to balance things out."

Ashley smiled, which was no doubt what Katelyn had intended. "I'll see what I can do."

"Okay, let me make a few calls, and then I'm out of here," Katelyn said, grabbing her purse. "Do me a favor, though, and give Brayden a hug. I'm guessing he really needs that right about now."

Ashley nodded. And more than a hug, he probably needed someone to check that wound. Among other things. She was more than willing to do whatever it took to make sure he was all right.

"Don't worry about anything," Katelyn assured her. "I'll let myself out."

It was the green light Ashley was waiting for. She headed for his bedroom. She knocked first, just once and not very hard. When he didn't immediately answer, Ashley let herself in and made her way through the still-open door of the bathroom.

Brayden was definitely in the shower.

Naked, of course.

Not that she'd expected to find him dressed, but it was still a shock to see him in the buff. A first for her. Ironic, since she was carrying his child.

The garden-style shower was in the center of the

room. Not some muted patterned glass enclosing it. Clear. Crystal clear. Well, with the exception of the condensation that was already clinging to the sides. Still, it wasn't misty enough to obstruct her view.

And what a view.

Leaning slightly forward, he had his palms pressed to the glass. His head, down. The steamy spray pounded his back and neck. Water sheeted down every lean, hard inch of him.

He was everything she had imagined he'd be, and more.

Without taking her gaze away from him, Ashley peeled off her sweater. Her movement must have caught his eye because he looked up. He seemed surprised, but he didn't move. He stood there, staring at her through the drenched glass.

Modesty should have been an issue since she was essentially doing a strip show, but those few modesty-related insecurities faded by the time she made it to her bra and panties. She slipped those off, too, opened the shower door and stepped into the mist with him.

"If you're trying to distract me," he greeted, "it worked. I'm distracted."

Ashley brushed her mouth over his. "You're so easy."

"Sometimes. With you, anyway."

Even though he'd meant it to be humorous, that touched her. But then, she'd known all along that this,

whatever this was between them, was special. It wasn't just about a baby. Nor was it just about Colton. This was also about what they felt for each other.

He smiled at her. And mercy, this one brought out the big guns. Dimples. They were too wholesome to belong on that rugged face, and yet they fit. Wholesome and dangerous. A bad combination for firing her libido. Of course, everything about Brayden fired her libido.

She reached behind her and switched the hard jets of water to a gentle spray so she could take a good long look at his body. In addition to the nick above his eyebrow, which he'd probably gotten from the thick underbrush in the woods, there was that angry gash on the top on his right shoulder.

No underbrush scrape.

The gash had been caused by Hyatt's bullet. A thought so vile that she had to push it aside. She didn't want Hyatt to be a part of this. He was gone. Dead. And he was out of her life forever.

Sliding her hand onto his stomach and brushing her hip against his, she walked behind him.

He was just as interesting from the back as he was from the front.

Well, almost.

The front did have one distinct advantage.

"This gash needs a stitch or two." She lightly touched his shoulder and frowned. "You really should see a doctor."

She slid her fingers and gaze lower. To the quarter-inch scrape on his lower back. And lower. Not because there were any nicks or cuts. But because she was human and couldn't resist putting her hands on him.

He made a low, husky sound of approval. Then he turned and captured her in his solid arms. He didn't stop there. Brayden pressed her against the slick glass.

"This won't get you off the hook," she advised him. He skimmed his hand over her breast. Just enough to make her nipples tighten. "But that might."

The corner of his mouth lifted. Ashley was relieved to see that smile, to feel his touch, but she didn't let it completely distract her. "Promise me you'll see a doctor."

He lowered his head and pinched her right nipple with his teeth. Not hard. Just the right amount of pressure. "Is that all you think about?"

It took a moment to find her breath. It had stalled in her throat. "Not all."

"Tell you what—I'll get down on my knees and give you a kiss that'll make you forget all about doctors and stitches." He slid his hand around the back of her neck. "Heck, it'll make me forget about them, too."

Ashley lost the breath she'd fought so hard to find. And once she could speak, she made him an offer that she wasn't about to let him refuse. "Brayden, let me make you forget."

He released the nipple he'd just taken into his mouth and lifted his head.

Their eyes met.

Ashley moved to the side and reversed their positions. Their bodies were slippery and wet so he slid right into place, with his back against the glass.

She started with his mouth. Kissing him. His mouth wasn't hard. But it wasn't exactly soft, either. The word that came to mind was *generous*. He moved into the kiss slowly. Easing his lips over hers. Touching. And giving.

Definitely giving.

He kept the contact gentle. At first. He gave her bottom lip a nip. Teasing her. Arousing her.

And when he chose to deepen the kiss, he deepened the embrace, as well. Pulling her to him. Tightening his grip on the back of her neck. Sliding his fingers deep into her hair. Encircling her in his arm.

Mercy, those arms.

She'd been right about those. All strength. All power. And she was wrapped in them.

He continued to kiss her with that clever mouth. He tempted her, adjusting the pressure, moving, drawing out the pleasure until he eased apart her lips. He tasted. Simply tasted. No rough plunge with his tongue. But he took. That mouth definitely took. Leaving her breathless and wanting more.

Brayden gave her more.

He leaned her back, slightly, cradling her head in his hand. Readjusting their bodies until they pressed against each other. Her breasts against his hard mus-

cled chest. Their bare legs fitted so that his left knee was between hers.

Intimate, definitely. Since they were naked.

But not nearly as intimate as what he was doing with his mouth. The taste of him filled her and whispered through her. It reminded her that there were so many things she wanted to do to him.

When he tried to adjust his grip, to align their bodies, she pinned his hands to the shower wall and continued with the kisses. But she didn't confine them to his mouth. She kissed his neck. His chest.

A source of many recent fantasies.

The taste of him, his scent, the way he felt beneath her lips and against her tongue, fulfilled those fantasies and a few more.

"You're playing with fire," he let her know.

"Among other things."

He chuckled. Half amusement, half torture. And he groaned and laced his fingers with hers.

The muscles of his stomach quivered against her mouth, and she took a moment to kiss him and pleasure him. And pleasure herself. It worked. The heat from the steam and the fire in her blood rushed through her.

Suddenly, she wanted more.

A lot more.

Ashley released the grip she had on his hands and sank lower. Catching his hips, she slid a line of kisses from his navel to the top of his right thigh. Muscles

jolted there, too. And they didn't relax when she moved those kisses to the left, toward the center, and lower.

As he'd suggested, she went down on her knees. Well, one knee anyway.

"You wouldn't," she heard him say.

"I would."

And she did.

There was no need to moisten her lips. The water sheeting down them was all she needed. Ashley kissed the tip of his erection, slowly, thoroughly. Then she took him into her mouth.

Brayden could do little more than just hold on.

And even that was a challenge.

He slid his fingers into her wet hair. Not to bring Ashley closer. That wasn't possible. Nor to help her maneuver, either—she was doing just fine all by herself, thank you very much. No, he held on to her as an anchor, because it sure felt as if he were about to slip off the edge of the world.

Ashley didn't hurry while she made love to him with her mouth. She, well, dallied with her tongue, her lips. Even her hot breath. And it surprised Brayden that a word like *dallied* was even in his vocabulary. But then, she was teaching him a few things. About restraint. About torture.

About how amazing she was.

Just when he thought he could take no more and just when he thought *more* was exactly what he

wanted, Ashley slid back up his body. And touched and rubbed every inch of him in the process.

She found his mouth and kissed him, hard. She didn't stop there. Oh, no. She seemed to be on some kind of healing quest that just might kill him.

Or save him.

Catching his shoulders, she pulled him down with her. And down. Until they were both on the warm shower floor with the steamy water spewing over and around them. He turned to put her against the glass, but again she outmaneuvered him.

Not that he resisted.

He was up for just about anything she wanted to do to him, or with him.

Instead, Ashley put his back against the glass, and while still French-kissing him and while sliding her hand over his chest, she climbed onto his lap. Straddling him. Aligning their bodies in the best possible way. This time his erection found a place even hotter and wetter than the shower.

Her gaze met his. Somehow. She had a wild look in her eyes. Wild and determined. And she was beautiful. *So* beautiful. Her dark hair clinging to her face. The water streaming down her ivory skin. Her mouth, slightly swollen from the torrid war she'd waged on his body.

"This won't be clinical sex," she promised.

"And not pity foreplay, either."

"Nope. No pity at all. Just sex."

Wrong. It wouldn't be *just sex* either. It couldn't be. Not with the feelings and emotions between them.

They'd make love.

And whether Ashley realized it or not, it would change everything.

He couldn't resist. He had to touch her. Brayden slid his palm down the column of her throat to her breasts. He took a second to sample them again. To taste her. And he circled his tongue around her nipples.

Ashley threw her head back and moaned. Not an ordinary moan. One that seemed to call to every cell in his body to claim her. To take her. To make her his and his alone.

He answered that *call.* He moved his hand down her stomach and between her legs. He touched. Lightly. Testing her response and learning what she liked in the process. He slid his fingers across the sensitive little bud, slipped his index finger in even deeper and had the privilege of hearing her say a very naughty word.

"Ashley," he teased.

Her eyelashes fluttered up, and her wild gaze met his again. "You said my name."

It wasn't an accusation or a reminder. It had a pre-orgasmic hint to it. So, he touched her again, his finger going deeper until he found an even more sensitive spot.

While he repeated her name.

She gulped in her breath. Gasping. And he knew

he'd learned a lot about how to please her. He had her close, so close, but then she latched onto his hand and stopped him.

"I want to watch you," she said.

Brayden might have assured her that he wanted to do the same thing, if she hadn't eased down onto him. Except she didn't really *ease* down. With the sweet sensations and the primal fire flaming through him, she took an inch of him inside her.

Then, another.

And another.

Slowly.

While she watched. The delicate muscles of her body gripped and teased him. Took him. Until she had all of him inside her.

She didn't stop there.

Oh, no.

Ashley caught his hands. Locked their fingers together. She shoved his arms against the glass. Holding him in place. Not that he was going anywhere in the literal sense. But he had no doubt she was about to take him places. Well, one place anyway.

And she moved.

Oh, man.

Did she ever move.

Sliding forward. Against him. Creating the friction. Her hips thrusting. Slow, at first. Finding the rhythm. The *right* rhythm.

And then she went faster. Harder. The slick mois-

ture of her body working in perfect harmony with her tight, gripping muscles. With each stroke, each thrust, each push, she took him higher. Closer. She gave him more. More. More.

"Ashley," he said.

She didn't stop, but her gaze came to his. "Brayden," she gave him in return.

Just Brayden. But it was more powerful than the magic she was creating with their bodies.

He watched her repeat his name. Watched her mouth form the syllables. Felt the hard, frantic, rhythmic slide of his body into hers.

And he saw her go over.

Saw her surrender.

With his name still on her lips.

Her own name pounded through his head. And it was the only coherent thought he had when he let himself go.

Ashley. Ashley. Ashley.

Chapter Sixteen

She was in love with Brayden.

The thought seemed to come out of nowhere, and Ashley decided that it might be a good idea if the particular reflection would go back from where it came. In their case, love didn't fix everything.

It couldn't.

Because love couldn't undo the past that would always be between them.

She stared in the bathroom mirror, towel drying her hair, but her attention definitely wasn't on her appearance. Nor was it on Brayden, who was drying off behind her. Even though the sight of him wet and naked certainly provided a nice distraction from her suddenly troubling thoughts.

They'd just shared some incredible minutes in that shower. Unforgettable, life-altering minutes. And now she was in love with him.

Not necessarily a good thing.

Because Brayden hadn't said a word about being

in love with her. Nor would he. She could never mean
as much to him as Dana had.

"Why the frown?" Brayden asked, slipping on his
jeans. He went closer, caught her arms and dropped
a kiss on her bare shoulder.

It was a simple intimate gesture that warmed her.
It also went a long way to giving her the courage to
tell him what she'd just realized—that she was in
love with him—but then Ashley caught a glimpse of
his bare shoulder in the mirror. His wound wasn't
bleeding, but it needed attention.

Ashley opened the medicine cabinet, located
some antibiotic cream and a bandage, and she went
to work. Unfortunately, that put her face-to-face, and
practically mouth-to-mouth, with Brayden.

"Well?" he prompted. He skimmed his hands
down her torso to her waist. Even though she had a
towel draped around her, she could still feel his touch.

"You'll live," she assured him, pressing the bandage into place.

He brushed his mouth against hers. "And that's
why you were frowning?"

"No. The frown is a product of all these jumbled
feelings I have."

Brayden eased back slightly. "You're not having
doubts about the baby?"

"No. Heavens, no. I really want this baby. Not just
for Colton, but for me. He or she is already part of

my life." She paused, debating, but decided not to hold back. "*You're* part of my life."

He stiffened slightly. "I know what you're saying, Ashley. What you're concerned about."

Good grief.

It sounded like the beginning of one of those let's-take-this-one-step-at-a-time speeches. And if so, he was right. Absolutely, emphatically right. They did need to take this slowly, to give themselves time to heal. Time to adjust to all the changes in their lives.

But Ashley suddenly didn't want that time.

She wanted him to pull her into his arms and tell her that he loved her.

He didn't. He just stood there staring at her for several long moments.

"Let's get dressed so we can talk," Brayden suggested. "With you wearing just a towel, my mind keeps wandering to other things."

Because he smiled, so did Ashley. Eventually.

Oh, well. Brayden might never fall in love with her, but at least the sexual attraction was there. Mercy, was it ever there. And that was a start. For now, it had to be enough.

Since she wasn't sure if Katelyn was still in the house, Ashley dressed in the bathroom after Brayden went into his bedroom to find a clean shirt.

"Hey, how'd the Christmas trees get here?" Brayden called out several minutes later.

Curious about that herself, Ashley followed the

sound of his voice to the living room. And there they were. Not one but two trees. The nine-foot-tall blue spruce she'd ordered earlier was everything the vendor promised her it would be. Full, fragrant and perfect for the large corner space adjacent to the front window. The other tree was almost identical except for the fact that it was artificial.

"I wanted this for Colton," Ashley explained. "It's only five days until Christmas."

"But why two?"

"I thought he might like to keep the artificial one up for a while. You know, to extend the season since he spent most of the month in the hospital. But I didn't order decorations. Hopefully, you have some?"

"In the hall closet, top shelf. There's more on the second floor, but I'll get those. There's a lot of junk and renovation stuff up there, and I don't want you to trip over anything." He glanced around. "Where's Katelyn?"

"She must have let the delivery person in and then left. I think she was anxious to get home to Joe."

It was an anxiousness that Ashley could now appreciate. Katelyn was going home to her husband, to a man she loved. There was a lot to be said for that.

And speaking of love, Brayden turned to her, presumably to resume that conversation they'd started upstairs. But he didn't get out even one word before his cell phone rang.

"Hold that thought," Brayden insisted after a huff, and he went to answer it.

Ashley listened for a couple of seconds, to make sure it wasn't some emergency or something to do with Colton, but she soon realized it was Brayden's father. A checkup call to make sure he was okay.

To give Brayden some privacy, Ashley went to the hall closet and located the plastic storage box marked Christmas decorations. It was on the top shelf just as Brayden had said it would be. She hauled it down and used her elbow to shut the door.

And when she turned, she came face-to-face with a man wearing a stocking cap.

Startled, Ashley started to scream. But he quickly slapped his hand over her mouth. Before she could struggle, before she could attempt to fight him off, he shoved a gun to the side of her head.

IT TOOK BRAYDEN A WHILE to update his father and assure him that he was truly okay. Evidently, Garrett had blabbed about the shoulder wound, and his father wouldn't stop talking until Brayden had promised to see a doctor. And he had promised. Not because he was anxious about his shoulder, but because he was anxious to finish his conversation with Ashley.

There was so much to tell her.

Too bad he didn't have specifics in mind, but he was hoping to sort out his feelings while they had a heart-to-heart.

After yet another promise to this father that he would see a doctor, Brayden hung up the phone and went in search of Ashley. She was probably trying to round up the Christmas decorations from the closet.

"Ashley?" he called out when he got to the hall. The box of lights and ornaments was on the floor, and the closet door was open. But Ashley wasn't anywhere around.

He called for her again. Waiting. But she didn't answer. And it was the silence that set his heart pounding and put him on full alert.

Brayden automatically reached for his gun. It wasn't there. He'd left it in the bedroom before he'd taken a shower. Not good. Because he was afraid he might need it. He sprinted toward his room.

It was empty.

He looked on the bed for his gun. Gone. The shoulder holster was empty. Other than that, nothing else in the room seemed disturbed. Brayden grabbed a backup weapon from his closet and raced out of the room to find her.

"Ashley?" he called out, praying she would answer.

Nothing. Absolutely nothing. And he knew that the full alert was necessary after all.

His mind began to race with all sorts of possibilities. Bad possibilities. Scenarios that included everything from an accident that had left her unconscious to Hyatt Chapman returning from the grave.

"Ashley?" he repeated. Louder this time. The next time was even louder.

She still didn't answer.

Brayden paused a second to listen. For any tiny sound that would indicate where she was and what had gone wrong. And then his gaze landed on the side door. The one that led to the garage.

It was wide open.

Had Katelyn left it open? Had Ashley gone out there looking for Christmas decorations? Those were possibilities, but Brayden didn't think so. His instincts were screaming that something was terribly wrong.

Flattening his back against the wall, he peered around the corner. It was dark, only meager light filtering through from the house into the garage. The only thing he could see clearly was his car.

Not an ideal scenario.

Because if someone was holding Ashley, they could easily be using the vehicle for cover.

Again, Brayden listened for a sound, for any indication that she was in there. And he got it. A shuffle of movement. But not from the garage.

From the second floor of the house.

Probably from the room directly above him.

Repositioning his gun, Brayden rushed to the staircase. The three-foot-tall wooden security gate— the one he'd used to deter Colton from going to the rooms still under renovation—was lying on the floor.

Trying not to make a sound, Brayden eased up the

steps, all the while listening for any indication that Ashley was okay. She had to be okay.

The landing on the second floor was coated with dust, and Brayden could see the footprints even in the filmy light seeping up from the bottom floor. Not one set of prints but two. Two. Ashley's and a man's.

The sight of those prints sent his stomach to his knees.

Did those prints belong to Trevor Chapman or Miles Granville? Either was a possibility since both men were a threat. And he knew that now. Unfortunately, *now* was too late. Whoever it was, the person had Ashley.

Keeping his footsteps light and staying close to the wall, Brayden went to the first room. No door. Just a wide arched entryway. The hardwood floor was littered with painting supplies and scaffolding. But neither Ashley nor the man who had her was there.

It was empty.

There were three other rooms, including a bathroom, and each of those four doors were closed. Any one of them could be hiding Ashley and her kidnapper.

Brayden pulled in a hard breath, turned the knob of the door nearest to him and shouldered it open. He immediately ducked back against the wall and waited.

Nothing.

He glanced quickly around the corner. Like the other room, there were renovation supplies, but no

sign of Ashley. Brayden was about to move on to the next room when he spotted the footsteps in the dust. Smeared steps as if someone had tried to cover them up.

His gaze fired to the closet door.

Closed.

It was a huge walk-in space for what was supposed to be the master bedroom. A perfect hiding place. Or maybe the steps leading to it were simply a decoy. Something meant to throw him off so he could be ambushed from behind.

If so, it could be a trap.

Since his instincts told him that's exactly what it was, Brayden slipped back out of the room. Moving fast, he went to the last room at the end of the hall. A storage room, loaded with boxes and old furniture. In other words, a perfect hiding place.

No quiet push of the door this time. Bracing himself for whatever or whoever might come at him, Brayden kicked open the door.

It took him a moment to spot Ashley. She was there, in the shadows, standing between a hutch and a sofa. She was obviously terrified. But alive.

Thank God she was alive.

Miles Granville was behind her. His arm circled tightly around her waist. He was wearing gloves, a dark raincoat and a knit stocking cap that he'd shoved up to expose his face but not his hair.

He also had a gun pressed to Ashley's head.

A gun fitted with a silencer.

For Brayden, seeing that weapon nearly knocked the breath out of him. He forced himself not to react. Not to fire. Not to lunge for the man and kill him. But instead, Brayden assessed the situation as objectively as possible. As he'd been trained to do. But, of course, he couldn't be objective. Not about this.

Because *this* was about Ashley.

"I let myself in the back door after your sister left," Granville announced in the same tone he probably used for a normal greeting. "Heard the water running in the shower so I used that time to set things up. Good thing, too. It'll look more realistic this way. As if Trevor chased you throughout the house."

"Trevor?" Brayden repeated, trying to concentrate on disarming Granville. "What does he have to do with this?"

"Everything." Granville lifted a shoulder. "He's in your pantry right now. I borrowed an idea from his brother and incapacitated him with a stun gun. After I gave him an almost certain concussion. He never even saw my face. In fact, with the hard hit on the head, he might even suspect you're responsible."

"He's wearing Trevor's shoes and has his gun," Ashley supplied through clenched teeth. "He plans to set him up...for this."

Well, that explained the hat, gloves and coat. Granville was trying to minimize any fibers or DNA

evidence that he might leave in what he no doubt considered to be a crime scene in the making.

One way or another Brayden had to stop him.

"Trevor will be blamed for Ashley's murder," Granville confirmed. "And yours. Wouldn't want to leave you out of this. A man who would bed his own sister-in-law deserves whatever he gets—don't you think?"

"I'm thinking a lot of things," Brayden countered. "But that's not one of them."

Granville chuckled. "Then perhaps I should just show you what I have in mind? It won't be long-range, like the way I killed your wife. By the way, just so you know—that wasn't an accident. I wanted both Ashley and Dana dead. The only accident was that I got interrupted by a security guard before I could finish the job."

The hurt registered. In his heart. In his head. But Brayden couldn't undo what had already happened to Dana. What he could do, maybe, was prevent Ashley from getting hurt.

"Speaking of finishing the job, it's time. No more candles, clinic fires, rental vans or mysterious messages on her phone." Granville pushed the gun harder against Ashley's head. "Point-blank. Much more efficient."

"Wait!" Brayden practically yelled it, and his voice was laced with desperation.

He had to convince Granville to back away, to let Ashley go. And if not, he had to figure out a way to

kill the man so he couldn't hurt her. "There's no reason for you to do this. The man who assaulted you is dead."

"True. I suppose I should thank you for ridding the world of Hyatt Chapman. But there are reasons for removing Ashley, as well. Revenge. Justice. I would have done it sooner if she hadn't disappeared. And I tried to kill her just days ago, but you prevented that, didn't you? Good thing, though. Because it'll work out better this way."

Granville aimed the gun right at Brayden.

"Trevor will be blamed," Granville continued. "I'll shoot him and make it look like a suicide. Yada, yada, yada. Then, I'll slip out the back, and everything will be tied up in a neat little package."

"Not quite," Ashley mumbled.

Brayden saw the flash of rage in her eyes. He saw the muscles tighten in her arms and face. And he knew what she was about to do. He yelled for her to stop.

But it was too late.

She rammed her elbow into Granville's stomach. In the same motion she dove to the side. But she wasn't fast enough.

Because Granville pivoted his weapon toward Ashley and fired.

Chapter Seventeen

"Ashley!" she heard Brayden yell.

Only seconds before Granville's shot zinged through the air.

The bullet missed her by a fraction, slamming into the sofa. Bits of foam stuffing and fabric flew through the air and fell around her like snow.

"Get down, Brayden," she called out.

Ashley did the same. She didn't waste any time scurrying behind the sofa. She grabbed a rusted can of paint, the only thing she could reach, and pushed it in front of her so she could use it as a weapon. Or use it to knock the gun from Granville's hand before he could fire another shot at Brayden.

She heard Brayden dive to the side and prayed he'd found adequate cover. If there was such a thing. The room was crammed with assorted stuff, but none of it would stave off bullets. They were both at risk.

And the baby.

Especially the baby.

All because Miles Granville couldn't let go of the past.

It didn't seem a good time for a revelation. But heaven help her, it was. The life-and-death situation made her see things clearly. The past was the past, and it was time for her to move on. Time to start a new life with her baby.

Maybe even with Brayden.

Unfortunately, Granville might take that chance at a new start away from her.

Granville fired again. This deadly swoosh of sound didn't come close to her and that meant it'd likely gone in Brayden's direction.

Her heart jumped to her throat.

The adrenaline slammed through her.

And it took every ounce of her self-control not to come out from behind that sofa and pummel Granville. But that would be stupid. It would not only get her killed but Brayden, as well. Because he would almost certainly leave cover to try to protect her.

So, Ashley waited. With her heartbeat pounding in her ears. With her throat, dry as dust. With every muscle in her body, knotted.

There was a shuffle of sound. A slight movement, and she suspected that Granville had hidden behind something, as well. That would account for why Brayden hadn't returned fire. It had to be the reason.

Because she refused to believe that Brayden might be hurt and incapable of returning fire.

Another movement.

Frantic, fast footsteps.

And then Granville was there.

Right next to her.

This time, he didn't put the gun to her, but to her stomach.

"Move," he mouthed. "And your baby dies."

She froze.

Because Granville's finger didn't seem too steady on the trigger and because of the insane look in his eyes. He'd definitely gone over the edge, and there would be no reasoning with him. If he fired now, neither she nor her baby would be able to survive that.

"Help!" someone called out. "I need help."

Not Brayden. And not Granville.

It was Trevor.

Walking right into a trap.

"I'm bleeding. And the phones aren't working so I can't call for an ambulance." Not a fluent explanation. It was filled with gasping breaths. Definitely a man in pain. "Is anyone here?"

Granville pushed the gun harder against her. "We're upstairs," he answered.

Not a frantic shout or a rough snarl, but a slightly louder than average invitation.

It worked.

A moment later, Ashley heard Trevor's uneven, slow movements on the stairs. Not footsteps. He seemed to be crawling to get to them.

But she also heard something else. No light shuffle this time. Just a burst of movement.

Brayden launched himself over the back of the sofa.

He tackled Granville. Ashley backed up, hoping she'd get a chance to hit Granville, but with the tangle of bodies, she wouldn't risk hitting Brayden.

Granville outsized Brayden by a good thirty pounds, and he used that size to slam him against the floor. He didn't stop there. Before Brayden could reposition himself, Granville rammed his fist into the wound on Brayden's shoulder. Ashley heard Brayden's low growl of pain but still didn't have a clear angle at hitting Granville with the paint can.

"Stay down, Ashley!" Brayden yelled.

She had no plans to do that anytime soon. What she did intend to do was help him.

Brayden's fist connected with the man's jaw, but in the ensuing scuffle, Granville knocked Brayden's gun from his hand. It slithered across the hardwood floor. Ashley didn't waste any time. She went after it and scooped it up just as Trevor staggered into the room.

"What…"

But Trevor didn't finish. And Ashley certainly didn't have time to tell him to get out of the way. Granville reared up from behind the sofa. His gun already aimed. Brayden latched onto his arm.

But not before Granville pulled the trigger.

With Brayden yelling for her to get down, Ashley

hooked her arm around Trevor's waist and dove to the side, pulling them both to the floor. The bullet rammed into the wall in the exact spot where Trevor had been standing. Another second, and he would have been shot.

Granville reaimed.

She didn't waste any time and didn't bother untangling herself from Trevor.

This was the moment she'd feared since Dana's death.

The moment she'd prayed would never come.

But it was also the moment she'd trained for.

So that she could survive.

And one way or another, she would survive. She had too much to live for to allow Miles Granville to take it away.

Ashley turned the gun toward Granville and fired. Unlike the other shots, this was a deafening blast of sound. It echoed through the room. And the bullet sliced through Granville's right arm. His hand and his weapon jerked back from the impact.

It didn't stop him, though.

He made a feral sound of outrage. More animal than human. His face contorted into a grimace of agony and determination. Despite the blood and the pain, he braced his wrist so he could fire again.

At her.

Before she could reaim, Brayden came up off the floor and slammed his body into Granville's. They

crashed against the window, glass flying. But it was enough to off-balance Granville.

His shot missed her.

Ashley pushed herself away from Trevor and raced across the room to help Brayden. But she couldn't help. She could only watch. It was too risky to fire while they were embroiled in a fistfight.

"I'll kill her," Granville shouted. "So help me. I'll kill her and the kid, too."

Because she was watching Brayden closely, Ashley saw the change in his body, the change in his expression. Granville's threat seemed to give Brayden a new surge of energy, of determination.

Brayden's right fist came up, connecting hard with Granville's chin. Brayden didn't stop there. He launched another punch. And another. All slamming into Granville.

Until the man's gun dropped to the floor.

And Brayden still didn't stop.

When Granville brought up his hands to continue the fight, Brayden hit him harder. So hard that Granville's body flew against the wall.

Before he could launch himself at Brayden again, Ashley aimed the gun at Granville.

Granville's wild gaze darted around the room like a caged animal. His attention landed on the window. Was he thinking about jumping, so he could try to escape?

Ashley stepped closer. "Move and you're a dead man."

She didn't shout. There was no anger in her voice. Just a calm reckoning that she wouldn't let him get away.

Granville's gaze left the window and sliced back to her. He examined her eyes, carefully, while emotion knotted and contorted the muscles in his body. His examination didn't unnerve Ashley because she knew he would see only resolve there.

And he apparently did.

Cursing her and cursing Brayden, Granville lifted his arm in the air and surrendered.

BRAYDEN LISTENED to the howl of the police sirens.

A truly welcome sound.

The moment the officers rushed into the room, he gladly turned Granville over to them. Granville—Dana's killer. Ashley's stalker. And the man who'd irrevocably altered so many lives.

Granville's confession would almost certainly send him either to death row or to a life sentence in a maximum-security prison. Either way, the man wouldn't be able to hurt Ashley again.

Granville's confession had also done something else. It had caused Brayden's heart to ache. For Dana. Maybe the ache would always be there. But it was different now. It was in perspective. Dana was gone, but he wasn't, and neither was Ashley. Too bad that it had taken almost losing her for him to realize that.

"You're bleeding," Ashley muttered, her voice

frantic. She grabbed a shirt from a box of clothes and pressed it to his wounded shoulder.

More sirens. This time from an ambulance. The red lights blended with the blue ones from the cruisers, and the rays prismed around the room. Two officers put a still-cursing Miles Granville on a stretcher and got him out of there. Another was tending to Trevor Chapman.

No cursing from Trevor. He was too busy trying to thank Ashley for pushing him out of the way of Granville's bullet. While he was at it, the man was also vowing that he wouldn't go through with those charges of police harassment that he'd threatened to file.

It was routine chaos in some ways.

But in other ways, there was nothing routine about what had just happened.

"The medics are on their way up," one of the detectives informed Brayden.

Every inch of him throbbed, but Brayden wasn't complaining about any of his injuries. Ashley was right next to him. And alive. She was a little bruised, and it might be a while before she got past the terrifying moments that Hyatt and Granville had put her through.

But she was alive.

And so was their baby.

"This time you're *definitely* going to the hospital," Ashley insisted while she applied pressure to the wound. "And don't you dare disagree."

Brayden didn't. Couldn't. Not that he particularly felt his injuries required a doctor, but he didn't want to do anything else to put panic in Ashley's eyes. She already looked panicked enough.

"You're seeing a doctor, too," he countered.

"Of course I am. But I'm not the one with a gash on my shoulder. I'm not the one bleeding."

Because she was trembling, and simply because he wanted to touch her, he slid his hand over hers. "I'll be all right. Promise."

Brayden had so much to say to her, so much he wanted to tell her. But the frantic, racing footsteps outside the door let him know he was within seconds of being whisked away by the medics. The timing was lousy for that heartfelt talk he'd promised her.

"You saved my life," she whispered. She blinked back tears not very successfully. "Our lives," she corrected, moving his hand from hers to her stomach.

Brayden pulled her closer, touched his mouth to hers. "You saved my life, too."

And he meant it.

She had.

In more ways than one, Ashley had saved him.

Chapter Eighteen

Brayden found Ashley and Colton exactly where he expected to find them. In the living room, next to the piles of glittery fake snow.

He smiled.

Despite the fact that Christmas was long over, they'd kept up many of the decorations. A way of extending the season. And amid those decorations was Ashley's and Colton's favorite spot for their afternoon naps. It was always the first place Brayden looked when he came home for a late lunch to check on them.

Which was often.

Two months hadn't been nearly long enough for him to forget how close he'd come to losing her.

A lifetime might not be enough to forget that.

However, those nightmarish memories weren't the only reason he came home. Not even close. He came because these days, it was truly *home*.

Colton was nestled in Ashley's arms. Also rou-

tine. They were lying on the floor on his grand-mother's patchwork quilt, their heads directly beneath the fake Christmas tree. Colored lights twinkled and flashed in rhythm to some very tinny carols.

But there was nothing routine or fake about the warmth that went through him.

It was nothing short of a miracle.

Brayden touched Ashley's cheek, and her eyes fluttered open. She smiled. Not a tentative smile, but a welcoming one. She eased herself away from Colton but not before planting a soft kiss on his son's forehead.

"I gave the nanny a day off," she whispered.

Yes. He'd figured that out. In fact, she'd given the nanny numerous days off. Brayden didn't mind in the least, and judging from what Colton had told him, neither did he. It suited both of them just fine that Ashley had become such an important part of their lives.

"Want me to fix you some lunch?" she asked, keeping her voice low.

Brayden shook his head and helped her to her feet. "Are you up for some company?"

Her smile faded a little. "I guess. But is something wrong?"

"No. My family just dropped by."

"Your family?" Her smile dissolved completely. "All of them?"

"All of them."

He didn't explain. Looping his arm around her waist, Brayden led her to the kitchen where the O'Malley clan was quietly waiting.

Garrett—sporting a few nicks and bruises courtesy of a recent undercover assignment—was munching on some leftovers he'd confiscated from the fridge. Katelyn and Joe were practically wrapped around each other. And finally there was his mom and dad, arms linked, they stood there.

Waiting.

All looking as anxious and concerned as Ashley.

Ashley smoothed her hand through her hair, obviously trying to fix it. She also closed the laptop that she'd left on the table and straightened some papers involving her latest case.

"What's going on?" Ashley mumbled, aiming her mumble at Brayden.

"We'd like to know the same thing," Garrett confirmed, after he tackled another spoonful of chili.

"Dr. Ellison called," Brayden explained, not able to hold back the surprise any longer. "She got the test results a couple of days earlier than expected."

Brayden's surprise caused everyone to hold their breaths. Because they knew this was the doctor who'd done the amnio to test the baby's bone marrow.

"We have a match," Brayden announced.

The silence and breath holding ended immediately, and the room came alive again. Shouts of joy.

Squeals of delight. Brayden celebrated right along with them.

During the wait for the results, he hadn't dared let himself hope too much. But the waiting was over. Finally. Colton had a donor. Soon his son would be well, and he'd become a father again.

He was very much looking forward to it.

"Is there a party?" he heard Colton mumble.

He looked over his shoulder to see the boy in the doorway. Colton was rubbing his still-sleepy eyes.

Brayden scooped him up in his arms. "Yep. It's a party."

His mother latched onto Ashley, and Brayden watched as each of his family members passed her around for hugs and kisses. She was smiling, then laughing, while the tears streamed down her face.

The moment was perfect.

Well, almost.

"Why're we having a party?" Colton wanted to know.

"We're celebrating. Because you're going to get well. Guaranteed. And there's also a bonus—you're going to become a big brother."

That cleared the sleepiness from Colton's eyes. "Really?"

"Really," Ashley assured him, walking closer. "I'm going to have a baby, and he or she will be your little sister or brother."

Colton's forehead wrinkled. "Not a pretend one,

though, right? 'Cause if it's pretend, that'd make it like a doll, and I'd ruther have a puppy than a doll. A spotted one with brown eyes."

"This baby is definitely not a pretend one," Ashley assured him. "It'll be the crying, diapers-required kind. Promise."

Brayden placed her hand on her stomach. "The baby's in here. Growing. You'll get to see him…or her in about seven months."

He hadn't expected anyone to let that last comment go unnoticed.

And it was noticed all right.

Ashley's gaze fired to his. So did the rest of the family's. In fact, the only one not staring at Brayden was Colton. He still had his attention focused on Ashley's stomach and was asking a question about how the baby managed to get in *there*.

Brayden would answer that one later.

"The amnio would have revealed the sex of the baby," his mom commented.

Joe nodded in agreement.

"And I'm sure Dr. Ellison wouldn't have kept that from you." That from Katelyn.

"Not a chance," his father piped in, walking closer, as well. "The doctor would have told you something as important as that."

"So, spill it," Garrett insisted. He strolled next to his sister and father. "Are we buying pink or blue badges this time around?"

Brayden ignored them all and looked at Ashley. "Would you like to know?"

She eagerly nodded and made a duh sound. "Of course."

"Okay." He handed Colton to his father and instead scooped up Ashley. He headed for the hall.

"Wait a minute." Not said by one of them, but by several. Garrett's voice, however, was the loudest. And it was Garrett who continued. "This is something we should all hear since it's a family thing. This kid is the newest O'Malley."

Brayden shook his head, disagreeing. "I figure Ashley should hear the news first. She is after all the mother of *this newest O'Malley.*"

Ashley's expression was part smile, part surprise, but in it was mixed a little apprehension. "Please tell me you're not carrying me because something is wrong?"

"Nothing's wrong. Everyone's healthy. And soon Colton will be, too."

The apprehension didn't completely fade. "So, why are you carrying me?"

"It's a primitive reaction." He took her into the living room and sank down onto the floor next to the Christmas tree. "A sort of me-man, you-woman. I carry you because you're carrying my child."

Apprehension vanished. She put her tongue in her cheek. "I didn't think you had primitive reactions."

He lifted an eyebrow.

"Other than *those* reactions," she amended, smiling.

Because Brayden wanted the feel of that smile on his mouth, he kissed her. Hard and long. Until they were both breathless and wanting more.

But then, he always seemed to want more of her.

"I think I'm having some of those primitive reactions of my own." Ashley buried her face against his neck. She brushed a kiss there, just below his ear and had his pulse jumping. "Not a good idea with your entire family in the kitchen. Besides, you have something to tell me. Something about the gender of our little O'Malley."

"I have lots to tell you. For starters, I love you."

Her head whipped up, her gaze racing to meet his. "Excuse me?"

"I love you," Brayden repeated. "And I want you to marry me."

Her breath shuddered. Not apprehension. Just the opposite. Happiness flooded through her eyes. Her face. Her smile.

Almost perfect.

Almost.

"You're already in my heart," Brayden told her. "Occasionally in my bed. But I want you there a lot more often. Every night as a matter of fact. Here, in our home."

She blinked. Her only reaction. "Yes."

Brayden did some blinking of his own. He'd ex-

pected Ashley to hesitate at least a little, but was thankful that she hadn't. "Yes to which part?"

No hesitation again. "To all of it."

He tamped down the relief, and the happiness, just long enough to make sure. "You didn't even have to think about it?"

Ashley shook her head. "No. I'm in love with you. And marrying you, moving in here with Colton and you, that's exactly what I want."

Even he couldn't hold down the happiness after hearing that. "Back up to that *I'm in love with you* part. It's true?"

Another duh sound. "Of course. Absolutely, emphatically, completely true. It's that forever kind of love, too. So, you should expect all sorts of mushy behavior from me."

He smiled, loving the sound of that. "Define mushy."

With a teasing look in her eyes, Ashley climbed onto his lap and whispered a very naughty suggestion. One that had him toying with the idea of sending his family on an errand so he could haul her off to bed. Or the shower.

Later, he'd do just that.

"This is perfect," she whispered.

Not quite. But soon.

"Well?" Garrett called out from the other room. "Pink or blue?"

Brayden ignored him. "That leaves the ring. Which I just happen to have." He leaned over, pulled

one of the branches from the tree and slid off the diamond engagement ring. The platinum and fiery stone had blended in perfectly with the twinkling lights and decorations.

Her eyes widened. "When did you put it there?"

"Weeks ago. I was just waiting for the right moment to ask you." He paused only long enough to kiss her. "It's the right moment, Ashley."

Brayden slipped the ring onto her finger. "I'm thinking about a short engagement. Very short. In fact, I'm thinking about this time next week, I'd like to wake up in bed with you as my wife."

Another smile. And no hesitation. "I'd like that, as well—both the wife part and waking up together. That'll include sex, too, right?"

"Oh, yeah. Lots of it."

"We're waiting." Katelyn this time.

Ashley pulled back slightly and looked at him. "Well? Which is it—pink or blue?"

Brayden didn't even try to fight back a smile of his own. "Both."

Her mouth dropped open. She tried to say something, but her first attempt failed. Ashley only managed a few stuttered syllables.

"Twins?" she finally got out.

"Twins," he confirmed.

He waited a moment, for Ashley's smile to catch up with his. Long enough for her to shriek with joy and launch herself back into his arms.

And Brayden kissed her long and hard. It was the exact moment he'd waited for.

Now, everything was perfect.

* * * * *

Don't miss the next exciting title
by Delores Fossen!
MOMMY UNDERCOVER
Harlequin Intrigue #829.
Available February 2005!

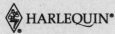
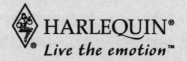

Like a phantom in the night
comes an exciting promotion from

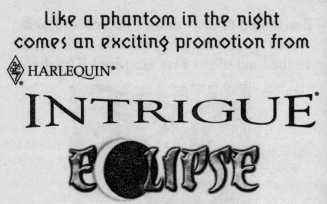

HARLEQUIN®

INTRIGUE®

ECLIPSE

GOTHIC ROMANCE

Look for a provocative
gothic-themed thriller each month
by your favorite Intrigue authors!
Once you surrender to the classic
blend of chilling suspense and
electrifying romance in these
gripping page-turners, there will
be no turning back....

Available wherever Harlequin books are sold.

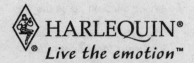

HARLEQUIN®
Live the emotion™

www.eHarlequin.com

HIE3

Bestselling fantasy author Mercedes Lackey turns traditional fairy tales on their heads in the land of the Five Hundred Kingdoms.

Elena, a Cinderella in the making, gets an unexpected chance to be a Fairy Godmother. But being a Fairy Godmother is hard work and she gets into trouble by changing a prince who is destined to save the kingdom, into a donkey—but he really deserved it!

Can she get things right and save the kingdom? Or will her stubborn desire to teach this ass of a prince a lesson get in the way?

On sale November 2004.
Visit your local bookseller.

LUNA™

Visit Dundee, Idaho, with bestselling author

brenda novak

A Home of Her Own

Her mother always said if you couldn't be rich, you'd better be Lucky!

When Lucky was ten, her mother, Red—the town hooker—married Morris Caldwell, a wealthy and much older man.

Mike Hill, his grandson, feels that Red and her kids alienated Morris from his family. Even the old man's Victorian mansion, on the property next to Mike's ranch, went to Lucky rather than his grandchildren.

Now Lucky's back, which means Mike has a new neighbor. One he doesn't want to like…

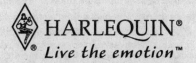

Live the emotion™

HSRH001204

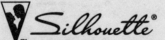

Dear Harlequin Intrigue Reader,

Our romantic suspense lineup this month promises to give you a lot to look forward to this holiday season!

We start off with *Full Exposure*, the second book in Debra Webb's miniseries COLBY AGENCY: INTERNAL AFFAIRS. The ongoing investigation into the agency's security leak heats up as a beautiful single mom becomes a pawn in a ruthless decimation plot. Next up…will wedding bells lead to murder? Find out in *Hijacked Honeymoon*—the fourth book in Susan Kearney's HEROES, INC. series. Then Mallory Kane continues her ULTIMATE AGENTS stories with *A Protected Witness*—an edgy mystery about a vulnerable widow who puts her life in an FBI special agent's hands.

November's ECLIPSE selection is guaranteed to tantalize you to the core! *The Man from Falcon Ridge* is a spellbinding gothic tale about a primitive falcon trainer who swoops to the rescue of a tormented woman. Does she hold the key to a grisly unsolved murder—and his heart? And you'll want to curl up in front of the fire to savor *Christmas Stalking* by Jo Leigh, which pits a sexy Santa-in-disguise against a strong-willed senator's daughter when he takes her into his protective custody. Finally this month, unwrap *Santa Assignment*, an intense mystery by Delores Fossen. The clock is ticking when a desperate father moves heaven and earth to save the woman who could give his toddler son a Christmas miracle.

Enjoy all six!

Sincerely,

Denise O'Sullivan
Senior Editor
Harlequin Intrigue

"I don't want t̶̶̶̶̶̶̶̶̶̶̶̶̶̶̶̶̶̶̶ Christmas," h̶̶̶̶̶̶̶̶̶̶̶̶̶̶̶̶̶̶̶̶̶̶̶̶̶̶̶̶̶̶̶̶̶̶̶ **might not be a̶̶̶̶̶̶̶̶̶̶̶̶̶̶̶̶̶̶̶**

"Santa *will* find you," Ashley promised. "I'll make sure of it."

He considered that with his now-pensive green eyes. Ashley had seen those eyes before. Brayden's eyes. It stirred at least a dozen new emotions seeing them on a child she loved.

Then Brayden was there, in the doorway, watching them.

"I want you to accept my offer to stay at my house," he said softly. "You might think I'm a couple of steps below navel lint, but I didn't ask you to come here so you could get hurt."

So, he didn't dismiss her fears of the stalker. Didn't give her one of those icy cop glances. It was one nearly perfect moment in what had been far from perfect between them.

And Ashley knew exactly where this had to go. Maybe she'd always known, but she'd needed this visit with her nephew for it to sink in. Now, she only hoped she could live with the decision she was about to make.

"I'll do it," she heard herself say. "I'll have your baby."